# LEMONS

## MELISSA SAVAGE

A YEARLING BOOK

Text copyright © 2017 by Melissa Savage
Cover art copyright © 2017 by Lydia Nichols

All rights reserved. Published in the United States by Yearling, an imprint of Random House Children's Books, a division of Penguin Random House LLC, New York. Originally published in hardcover in the United States by Crown Books for Young Readers, New York, in 2017.

Yearling and the jumping horse design are registered trademarks of Penguin Random House LLC.

Visit us on the Web! rhcbooks.com

Educators and librarians, for a variety of teaching tools, visit us at RHTeachersLibrarians.com

The Library of Congress has cataloged the hardcover edition of this work as follows:
Name: Savage, Melissa (Melissa D.), author.
Title: Lemons / Melissa Savage.
Description: First edition. | New York : Crown Books for Young Readers, [2017]
Summary: After her mother dies in 1975, ten-year-old Lemonade must live with her grandfather in a small town famous for Bigfoot sightings and soon becomes friends with Tobin, a quirky Bigfoot investigator.
Identifiers: LCCN 2016037977 | ISBN 978-1-5247-0012-6 (hc) |
ISBN 978-1-5247-0013-3 (glb) | ISBN 978-1-5247-0014-0 (ebook)
Subjects: | CYAC: Mystery and detective stories. | Yeti—Fiction. | Friendship—Fiction. | Individuality—Fiction. | Single-parent families—Fiction. | Orphans—Fiction. | Grandfathers—Fiction.
Classification: LCC PZ7.1.S2713 Lem 2017 | DDC [Fic]—dc23

ISBN 978-1-5247-0015-7 (pbk.)

Printed in the United States of America

10 9 8 7 6 5 4 3

First Yearling Edition 2018

Random House Children's Books supports the First Amendment and celebrates the right to read.

*For my son*

# CONTENTS

# 1

# ONE WOOLLY MONSTER
# AND A WEIRDO KID

Bigfoot.

It's the very first thing I see when we pull into town. A gargantuan wooden statue of the hairy beast, stuck right smack in the middle of the square, like he's the mayor or President Ford or someone real important like that.

"Where are we, anyway?" I ask the social worker who came to get me all the way down in San Francisco.

I've only met her once before this and I can't remember her name. I think it starts with a W. Maybe an M. There were two of them who came to visit. I can't remember the other lady's name either. This one must have drawn the short straw to have to drive me all the way up to this Podunk place.

"We finally made it, Lemonade." Her eyes meet mine in the rearview mirror. "They say Willow Creek is the Bigfoot capital of the world."

"You mean like that thing actually lives here?"

She smiles and makes a left turn down Seventh Street. "We're almost there, should be just up this way a piece."

This place is nothing like home. And I already know I'm going to hate it.

Tall pines instead of skyscrapers, dirt instead of sidewalks, and one woolly monster lurking somewhere in the forest. With my luck, his main food source is ten-year-old girls.

"I want to go home," I mutter under my breath. "Why couldn't I have just stayed with my teacher?" I call up to the front seat. "Miss Cotton said she loves having me there. She even told me so."

"I'm sorry, Lemonade," she says, keeping her eyes on the road this time. "I'm afraid that's not an option right now. There would have to be forms completed for that to happen permanently."

"She would do that," I tell the lady. "She always has our papers corrected by the very next day. Just ask her, she'll tell you."

"I've already spoken to her about it, honey," she says. "Believe me, if things change, you'll be the first to know."

"I'll make sure and remind her. She promised to call me sometimes and write me letters, too. At least until I get to go back."

This time the lady doesn't say anything.

I lay my head back on the seat and stick my arm out the window. The warm summer air grabs it, and my hand hangs ten on a wind wave. I breathe in deep.

It smells like grass.

Dirt.

And bugs.

At home, the air smells like ocean mixed with car exhaust and the glorious crispy fried egg rolls from Mr. Chin's restaurant on the corner. He makes the best egg rolls in town. The sign in the window even says so.

The sky is a fire orange, even though the sun is just about out of sight behind the trees, leaving long, dark shadows between the pines that line the road.

Which is the reason why I almost miss him.

Some weirdo kid darts through the trees with binoculars hanging from his neck.

He's wearing a floppy tan safari hat folded up in front and held on by a strap under his chin. Across the underside of the brim are some kind of hand-painted letters. I can tell they say something real important, too, because why else would you have hand-painted letters anywhere?

But he's running so fast I can't read what they say.

## 2

# THE SECOND-WORST
# DAY OF MY LIFE

"Lemonade," the old man says slowly, like he's trying it on for size.

He eyes me from under unruly gray eyebrows in the front hall of one of the old farmhouses lined up on Seventh Street.

The lady turned up the driveway of the medium-sized white one with yellow shutters on it. We walked up five wooden steps and onto a great big porch wrapped all around it, with a bright yellow swing just to the left of the front door.

Inside, it's nothing like our apartment in the city—it's cold and dark and smells like old books and coffee beans. At home we live on the third floor of a Victorian walk-up. Mama painted every wall pink and hung white fluffy curtains at all the windows and there were always fresh daisies on the kitchen counter except in the winter. She had the record player going all the time too. Usually Simon and Garfunkel or Cat Stevens and sometimes James Taylor.

This place doesn't have anything playing, not a television set or a radio or anything. And the walls are just plain white ones with only boring wooden blinds at the windows.

"We meant to get here by four, but the traffic in the city was awful," the social worker tells the man.

It's weird that I can't remember her name, since we only drove for six whole hours to get to this place. We even played a round of the alphabet game until my eyelids got so heavy I couldn't keep them open anymore. I was winning up until then, after spotting a Q on a liquor store sign outside Redding.

"Not a problem," the man tells her, continuing to eye me.

I eye him right back.

He's missing the middle part of his hair, like someone divided his head up into thirds and subtracted the center.

I'm real good at math. I got an A in Mr. Mahoney's math class, and everyone knows Mr. Mahoney gives the hardest tests at Sherman Elementary.

"Lemonade," the man says again, running a hand through one of the thirds of hair that's still there. It's black and wavy with speckles of gray mixed in. There's a short beard right around his mouth that has even more gray in it than the ring around his head. He has on a checkered short-sleeved shirt and long tan shorts with hiking boots and tall white socks that come up to his knees.

"Lemonade Liberty Witt," I say, standing straight. "Lem for short. I'm ten and three quarters. I'll be eleven on September sixth."

"Uh-huh." He pulls horn-rimmed glasses from the checkered shirt pocket and slips them across his nose to examine me some more. There's a bright silver ring on his finger. "Small for ten and three quarters, aren't you?"

He's full of the kinds of questions that don't seem to want answers.

So he doesn't get one.

I cross my arms and glare at him instead.

"Same green eyes . . . and"—he clears his throat—"those red curls."

I swallow hard.

"Can you tell us where Lemonade will be staying while she's here, Mr. Witt?" the lady asks with a straight-lipped smile stretched across her teeth.

He sighs and stuffs his glasses back in his front pocket. "This way, second door on your right," he grumbles, making his way down a dark hall just past the kitchen. "Grab your suitcase," he calls over his shoulder.

My fingers curl around the handle of Mama's pink suitcase, but the lady waves my hand away and grabs it for me. I follow it, my eyes fixed on the bouncing red tag that's tied to the handle with a bright orange and green crocheted yarn braid. It has Mama's handwriting on it.

*Elizabeth Lilly Witt*
*245 Ashbury Street, Apt. 3095*
*San Francisco, California*

The wooden floorboards in the hall groan under each step, and there's a loud ticking from a clock somewhere in the house. The plain white walls in the hall are filled with crooked-hanging picture frames telling the story of a happy family.

The house is quiet.

Too quiet.

There are no sounds of traffic or honking horns or bustling feet of people on their way to their office. There's not even any opera singing from Miss Kay in 3096, practicing for her evening performance at the San Francisco Opera.

Just a moaning floor, a ticking clock, and the sound of my own pulse pounding against my temple.

I stop just outside the second door on the right and peek inside. This can't be it. Maybe he meant the third door on the left.

I watch the social worker plop Mama's suitcase on top of a blue and green wool blanket that's pulled tight across a single mattress. There's a ratty trunk at the end of the bed and a wooden chest of drawers with bronze handles in a far corner. An old radiator sits under the window with cobwebs near the floorboards, and a hundred dull-looking grown-up books line a wall of bookshelves.

"It's my study," the old man says like it's an apology. "It's the best I could do on such short notice. . . ." His voice trails off into a whisper, and he clears his throat again. "I had no idea . . ."

"It's just fine," the lady says. "Lemonade, why don't you put some of your things in the drawers while I talk with your grandfather."

*Grandfather.*

He must be a mind reader too, because he clears his throat

a bunch more times and says, "You can call me Charlie," before making his way out the door.

She follows him, her lips in the same straight-line smile, but before she closes the door, she meets my eyes one more time.

"I'll be back to check on you each month," she says.

I don't say anything.

"It's going to be okay," she tells me. "It really is."

Except I don't know who she's trying to convince.

"No, it's not," I tell her. "It's never going to be okay ever again."

She smiles that kind of smile like she thinks she understands me even though I know she doesn't.

No one does.

Except maybe Miss Cotton and all my friends at home. They understand because they were there on the single worst day of my entire life. I bite the inside of my cheek to keep the tears from dropping and watch her slowly pull the door closed behind her. I sit down next to Mama's suitcase. The blue and green wool blanket itches me on the backs of my legs.

Delores. Delores Jaworski. That's her name.

I sure hope the next time I see her she has those papers she was talking about because there's no way I can stay here.

There's no fluffy down comforter with a big, beautiful rainbow on it like the one I have at home. And no plastic stars on the ceiling that glow when the lights are off. And there's not even a warm, fuzzy rug in the middle of the floor for cold mornings.

This floor is bare naked.

This has to be just one big, horrible mistake. It's got to be. A miserable nightmare that I'll wake up from at any moment.

I want to cry and scream and run. I want to run until I make it all the way back home.

My forearm wipes at the tears that find their way down my cheeks. I touch the red tag on the handle and finger the bright orange and green crocheted yarn braid that holds it in place.

"Elizabeth Lilly Witt," I whisper. "Why did you leave me?"

# 3

# BIRD FOOD FOR BREAKFAST

"Mama gets me Life cereal," I inform Charlie at breakfast the next morning. "And she always has Twinkies in the cupboard for my afternoon snack."

"Mmmm-hmmm," he says, setting down the *Two Rivers Tribune* and grabbing a box with the words *Nature's Bran* on it.

He pours it into the blue ceramic bowl in front of me. I watch sticks and seeds and bark drop from the box. There's a carton next to him and he splashes some milk on top. Skim.

"We use two percent," I tell him.

He doesn't say anything this time, just picks his newspaper back up and starts reading again.

On the front page is an article about the Vietnam War finally coming to an end.

I sigh and chew the bark.

He sips his coffee.

Black. No sugar.

I wonder what my very best friend, Erika Vass, is having for breakfast. I bet it's not bird food. Erika lives two buildings over from us on Ashbury. She is the best dancer in our dance class, she always lets me eat the whipped cream off her dessert when she orders hot lunch in the school cafeteria, and she has a dog named Dr. Pepper that we walk together after school.

"Charlie! Charlie!"

Footsteps pound the front porch steps, and the screen door slams. A boy all out of breath darts into the kitchen, stopping right in front of the old man.

The same boy from the pines.

Except, instead of binoculars, today he has a movie camera hanging from his neck.

Gold wire-rimmed glasses sit low on his nose and a mound of reddish-brown curls sticks out from under the safari hat, which is still strapped tight under his chin. On the hat is the same stupid hand-painted sign that I couldn't read before. But this time I can see the shaky black letters just fine.

## BIGFOOT DETECTIVES INC.

"Morning, Tobin." The old man smiles at him. An actual, real smile with teeth and everything.

"I really think I got it this time!" The boy is holding a canister of movie film high in the air like a trophy. "Can you drop it off at the Fotomat to get developed before you open up the store this morning?"

"Good for you!" the old man cheers. "Of course I can. Hand that thing on over here."

"Thank you, Charlie," the boy says, pulling a chair out and sitting down next to me.

I stare at the kid, waiting for him to say something to me. But he doesn't. He pours sticks and seeds and bark into a blue bowl for himself like he doesn't even care that it isn't Life or Cheerios.

"What did you get?" I ask him.

The boy peers at me over his wire-rims like he didn't even notice that I've been sitting right next to him this entire time. Blue eyes with little specks of brown in them examine me top to bottom.

"Who are you?" he demands.

"Hasn't anyone ever told you that it's rude to answer a question with a question?" I say.

The boy looks at Charlie and then back at me.

"This is Lemonade Liberty Witt," the old man tells him, folding up his newspaper. "You can call her Lem. Lem, this is Tobin Sky. He lives right across the street. And he's Willow Creek's very own Bigfoot detective."

Like I can't read his stupid hat for myself.

"Is that a joke?" I snort, and a little skim milk comes out of my nose.

"Nope." Tobin Sky pops up and sticks his hand in the front pocket of his khaki shorts. "I'm the official investigator of any and all sightings here in Willow Creek." He pulls a small crumpled piece of paper out and hands it to me. "My card," he says in a very official-sounding way.

I inspect it.

## BIGFOOT DETECTIVES INC.
### Handling all your Bigfoot needs since 1974
### Tobin Sky: 555-0906

"*All your Bigfoot needs?*" I read out loud.

"That's right. And, ah, actually . . ." He points at the card in my hand. "I'm going to need that back when you're done with it." He pushes his glasses up the bridge of his nose with his pointer finger. "It's my only one."

# 4

# INTERPLANETARY TRAVELER

I think I've moved to Jupiter.

Maybe Mars.

It's not just that there's a wooden statue of a Bigfoot in the center of town. Or that there's an actual resident Bigfoot hunter running around with a single business card stuffed in his pocket. To top it all off, the old man even owns a shop out on Highway 299 called Bigfoot Souvenirs and More.

Which I find out is where he goes after breakfast every day but Sunday.

After this morning's bowl of bird food, we watch him from the front porch as he backs an old maroon station wagon named Jake out of the driveway and putters down Seventh Street.

"What's with this town?" I ask Tobin after the car takes a left at the stop sign and disappears around the corner.

"What do you mean?"

"All this Bigfoot hullabaloo."

He looks at me again, this time with his eyebrows wrinkled together.

"It's not hullabaloo," he says real serious-like. "It's true. Haven't you heard of the footage they got out this way eight years back?"

I shake my head.

"The Patterson-Gimlin film?"

"Nope." I examine my peeling nail polish like I couldn't care less.

Which I couldn't.

"They filmed a Bigfoot over at Bluff Creek on October twentieth, 1967," Tobin says, taking a seat on the yellow porch swing.

I look up. "You mean . . . it's really true?"

"Of course it is. You think I'm making this up?" he says, like *I'm* the crazy one. "And since that time, there have been hundreds of sightings all over. But no one else has caught one on film . . . until now." He holds up his camera to show me. "I'm going to be the very next one to do it. Patterson, Gimlin, and Sky. I'll be on the Channel Four News and everything."

I watch him huff hot air on the lens and wipe it with the bottom of his red T-shirt. Then he squints through the viewfinder, pointing it in all different directions.

Left, then right.

Right, then left.

Up, then down.

He huffs more air and wipes again.

I go back to my fingernails.

After I finish scraping all the polish off my pinky, I look at him again. "So, can I ask you a question?"

He doesn't say anything, like he's too busy concentrating on his lens to even bother with me.

"If they're really real, why is it so hard to find them?" I ask anyway.

"Who?" He looks up.

"Who do you think? The Bigfeet."

"Foot," Tobin corrects.

"What?"

"You don't say *feet*. It's *foot*. Big*foot*. Singular, not plural." I roll my eyes.

"Big*foot*," I say. "Why is it so hard to find them? What are they hiding from?"

He puts the camera down and stares straight ahead, chewing on his bottom lip.

"People," he finally says, and starts squinting through the viewfinder again. Except this time he points the thing right at me.

"Why do they hide from people?" I ask the lens.

Tobin lowers the camera into his lap and focuses on his dark blue sneakers. "'Cause people can hurt you."

I don't say anything.

We sit on the swing in silence as he continues to huff and wipe. When he seems content that the lens is the way he wants it, he turns to me again.

"Want to see something?"

I shrug. "I guess."

"First, you'll have to take an oath of ultimate secrecy," he warns me.

"For what?"

"Can't say. You have to swear ultimate secrecy for eternity or longer before I can disclose any further top secret information. Can you do that?"

"What's longer than eternity?"

"What?"

"Eternity *is* the longest. There's nothing longer than that." He sighs a blast of air in my direction.

"Can you promise you won't blab or not?"

# 5

# ONE HIGH-TECH OPERATION
# AND A BAG OF LAWN FERTILIZER

"This is the Bigfoot Detectives Inc. Headquarters," Tobin tells me over his shoulder, wiggling a key in the lock of Charlie's crumbling garage out back.

"I promised eternal secrecy for this?" I ask. "It's a garage. And barely even that. It's one Big Bad Wolf's blow away from being a pile of boards."

"That's just my cover." The key turns. "Outside it may look like your typical garage, but inside is a highly technical, totally confidential cryptozoological operation."

I give the place the once-over. There are shingles missing on the roof, and the white paint is peeling. I think it might even be leaning to the left a little.

Tobin turns to face me before he opens the door. "Ultimate secrecy," he repeats. "You promised."

"It was like five minutes ago—you don't think I remember?"

Tobin pushes the door open and a stifling, ripe stench slaps me in the face. An aromatic blend of baking garbage from the overflowing cans, gasoline from the lawn mower, and a bag of lawn fertilizer leaned up in one corner.

I hold my nose as he pulls a battered string hanging from the rafters. A single stark bulb shines down on a wooden desk in the back corner. It has a torn-up old copy of *Grant's Atlas of Anatomy* under one leg to keep it from wobbling. On the desk are one green phone, some kind of tape recorder, a rusty lamp, and a carved wooden sign with shaky letters on it.

## BIGFOOT DETECTIVES INC.
## TOBIN SKY, FOUNDER AND PRESIDENT

"This is your high-tech operation?" I pick up the wooden sign and study it.

"Charlie made me that for my birthday last year," Tobin informs me.

I set it back down.

He straightens it.

"What's that?" I point to the tape recorder next to the phone.

"That's an old answering machine from Charlie's office. Now that he's retired, he lets me use it. You know, so I don't miss any important sightings when I'm out on another call."

"Oh," I say. "So, who else is in this Inc. of yours?"

"What do you mean?" He slips the camera strap over his head and places the camera carefully on the desk.

"Inc.," I say again. "It stands for *incorporated*, right? More than one person? Who else is in your Inc.?"

"There isn't anyone else," he tells me, shuffling through a yellow legal pad filled with scribbles. "I don't need other people."

"So, you're saying it's just you, then?"

"Yep."

"Then it's not really an Inc. It's just you."

He looks at me.

"I guess." He shrugs. "I mean, unless . . . well . . ."

"What?"

"Nothing." He shuffles more papers in his yellow pad.

"No, what were you going to say?"

"I suppose . . . I mean, I guess I could use an assistant to help out . . . you know, summers can get busy with calls about sightings, encounters, and stuff like that. And of course there will be expeditions."

"So, you're saying you want me to be your Inc.?"

"Yeah, I mean, you know . . . only if you want to . . . you could . . . if you want."

I think about it.

"I guess I can be your Inc.," I tell him. "At least while I'm here."

Tobin stops shuffling his papers and looks at me over his glasses. "You're leaving?"

"That's the plan," I tell him, picking up a battered spiral notebook with the words *LOGGED SIGHTINGS* scribbled on the front of it. "I'm going home."

"When?" He takes the notebook from my hand and puts it back on the desk in the same place I found it.

"That's still a work in progress," I say, looking around the garage. "But one thing I know for sure is that I don't belong here."

# 6

# ORIENTATION

"If we're going to make you the official new assistant here at Bigfoot Detectives Inc., you'll need a new-employee orientation."

"Orientation to what, the mousetraps or those old fishing poles in the corner?" I look around again. "What else is there to know?"

"Well, for starters, you'll need to take the Bigfoot Detectives Inc. oath. Raise your right hand and repeat after me."

"I already promised the whole ultimate secrecy thing. Is this really necessary?"

He raises his right hand and waits for me to do the same.

I do, but only after I give him my very best eye roll.

"I, *Lemonade Liberty Witt, promise not to blab any top secret Bigfoot-related matters . . . ,*" Tobin says.

I repeat it.

*"To any source, including all newspaper and TV reporters, corporate spies, and any and all naysayers, while employed at Bigfoot Detectives Inc., for eternity or longer."*

"Give me a break."

*"Say it."* He peers at me over his wire-rims.

I say it.

"Good. Okay, now let me give you an orientation to the business." He taps his finger on his chin. "Let's see . . . well . . . this is where I keep the stapler." Tobin picks it up from on top of the desk to show me, then sets it back down.

Like I don't have eyes.

"The stapler remover." He holds that up too and then sets it back down next to the stapler.

"Okay, let me stop you there, because I can see where this is going," I say. "I thought this would be more about the meat and potatoes of the whole technical operation you've got happening here."

"We just had cereal," he says, looking at me funny.

"What? No. The Bigfoot *stuff*. I mean, what do you do, really?"

"I'm getting to that," Tobin says. "First things first. The message pad . . ." He holds up a pad that has the word MES-SAGES printed across the top and places it back on the desk.

"Are you kidding me?" I put my hands on my hips.

"These are all very important things to know," he explains. "What if a call comes in and I'm not here, and you don't know where the message pad is?"

"You mean this pad on top of the desk with the word *messages* on it?" I grab it.

"Well, sure, you know where it is now." He takes it from my hand. "And . . . ah, that's not really supposed to be moved unless there's an actual message." He puts it back in its spot.

"Is this a girl thing?" I ask. "Because I can do anything you can do. Just because I'm a girl doesn't mean the only thing I need to know is where the stapler is. I can do more than staple and unstaple."

"I know it," he says. "The magnetic paper clip tray." He holds it up for me to see.

I groan.

"What?"

"If I'm going to be a partner here, you need to tell me the stories. What you do. You know, like the real Bigfoot-type things that people call you about."

"Partner?" His eyebrows go up. "Who said partner? I don't remember saying anything about partner. I am the founder and president of Bigfoot Detectives Inc. Read the sign." He picks up the crudely carved wooden sign from the desk and points to it. "You will be my assistant. *Assistant.* I thought I made that perfectly clear."

"Maybe I want to be partner? *Witt-Sky Bigfoot Detectives Inc.* has a nice ring to it."

"Well, first of all, it would be *Sky-Witt* if anything, and, secondly, the only way I would ever make someone partner would be if it was someone who I knew was planning on staying for a real long time."

I don't say anything.

"You said you're leaving, right?" he asks. "Isn't that what you said?"

I think about it again and then pick up the stapler and a bunch of loose papers and staple them all together.

"Assistant it is," I say.

"Oh, ah, actually . . ." Tobin reaches for the papers in my hand. "Those aren't supposed to be stapled—"

The green phone jingles and Tobin dives for it, answering on the first ring. The papers go flying.

"Hello? Bigfoot Detectives Inc. This is Tobin Sky, lead detective. What Bigfoot concern may we help you with today?"

He grabs a pencil from a Styrofoam cup on the desk and begins to scribble furiously on his yellow legal pad.

"Uh-huh . . . uh-huh . . . ," he says between pauses. "Interesting . . . Of course we can come right away. . . . Yes, ma'am. . . . Thank you for calling, Mrs. Dickerson. . . . Good-bye."

He hangs up the phone and looks at me over his glasses with a big goofy smile on his face. He waves the yellow legal pad in the air.

"Your very first Bigfoot sighting! Are you ready?"

"Ready for what?"

"Only to change your life forever!" he says, tightening the chin strap on his safari hat.

I think about it.

"I guess," I say.

"There's been another sighting at Mrs. Dickerson's, and she needs us out there right away to lift some possible prints. You got a bike?"

I shake my head.

"That's okay. I'll give you a buck."

"A what?"

"You can ride on the handlebars."

"Uh, I have two words for you," I say. "They are *no* and *way.*"

He doesn't even hear me.

"Let's go!" he hollers with excitement, grabbing the handle of a black leather case and scrambling out the door.

# 7

# VERMIN APPETIZER

I can't feel my fingers, and my butt is dead asleep. I'm sure I've heard somewhere that these are the first signs of a heart attack.

Or maybe it was a stroke.

I'm white-knuckling the handlebars of Tobin's fire-engine-red bike, my butt smooshed between the tall silver bars and my legs outstretched in front of me while he drives like a lightning bolt through town. Houses and storefronts blend into the landscape in one gigantic blur on our way to Mrs. Dickerson's. Once we're past the tiny town, there are just lots and lots of vile-smelling grassy pastures filled with chewing cows that stare as we whiz by them.

And that's what I see when my eyes are open.

On the metal platform over the back wheel are Tobin's yellow legal pad and the mysterious black case he grabbed on his way out. They're strapped tight with a roll of twine he used from a shelf in Charlie's garage.

"That's Charlie's store! See it?" He points. "That wooden cabin with the green door!"

I peek open one eye.

"Both hands! Both hands!" I holler back at him, gripping even tighter and closing my eyes again.

Tobin takes a sharp right down a bumpy dirt road. We bounce and bumble over rocks and dips in the road until the vibration makes my lips itch. I scratch them with my teeth and silently repeat the parts of the Our Father prayer that I can remember from church. Mama and I only made it to church at Christmas and Easter, and sometimes Good Friday.

All I can remember is something about bread and trespassing, which doesn't really seem to fit this situation.

"See that little blue house up there on that hill?" Tobin says, pointing again. "That's Mrs. Dickerson's place."

I peek another eye open, but when I open my mouth to scream at him again about keeping his hands on the handlebars, nothing comes out. That's because something flies in instead. I cough and choke, but whatever it is takes a sharp left at a tonsil and dive-bombs down my throat, lodging in a kidney. Or maybe it's my liver.

I gag and try to spit, except when I do, it just splashes back at me, hitting me in the cheek.

"I just ate a bug!" I cry. "I swallowed the entire body of an insect! What's it going to do to me?"

"Oh, they can't hurt you," Tobin tells me. "Charlie says aphids are a good source of protein."

"Protein!" I gag again. "And what's an aphid, anyway?"

"Aphids are a group of various soft-bodied insects."

All the sticks and seeds and bark from this morning stand at attention, ready for their encore.

"I can feel it burrowing into my gallbladder!"

"It is not," Tobin says.

I think I hear him laughing, but my eyes are still closed, so I can't be absolutely sure.

I open them again when Tobin turns another corner and slows down. He pedals up the dirt drive of a small blue house with six windows on the front of it, three along the top and three along the bottom. There is a white flower box stuck to the bottom of every window, each one filled with bright red roses. And there's a round table on the front porch with a yellow tablecloth blowing in the breeze. The table is set with a vase of even more roses, china teacups with the saucers underneath, and a plate stacked high with fresh-baked cookies.

I know they're fresh-baked because I can smell the smell of baking cookies seeping out of the screen door.

Tobin stops the bike and holds it steady while I de-wedge my butt out from between his handlebars. My legs are noodles, and it feels like a million pins are poking me in my lower regions. I stomp my feet to wake everything up and use the sleeve of my T-shirt to wipe the boomeranged spit off my right cheek. I'm already full of dust and bug spit and it's only nine o'clock. The bath from this morning lasted me all of five minutes.

Charlie didn't have any bubbles, either. I had to use a big green bar of Irish Spring soap and a plain blue washcloth. I told him Mama gets me Mr. Bubble and a puffy pink sponge for my baths, but he didn't say one word.

"Mrs. Dickerson!" Tobin calls while he works to unknot the twine tied tight around his leather case and legal pad. When he finally gets them free, he dashes up the front steps, and I follow.

The new white tennis shoes that Mama and I got at Hanson's Shoes are dirty now too. I spit on my hand and rub a spot, but it just smears and only makes it worse.

I feel like crying.

But I don't.

Tobin bangs three loud knocks on the screen door. The cookies piled high on the plate smell glorious, and I can't help but stare at them.

Too bad I already filled up with vermin on the way over. I gag one more time just thinking of it.

"Mrs. Dickerson!" Tobin calls louder this time, peering through the screen between cupped hands.

"Oh, there you are, Tobin, sweetheart. Thank you for coming so quickly," Mrs. Dickerson's voice says from somewhere inside the house.

When she turns a corner, I can see she walks with a bright silver cane. We watch her slowly slide her way toward us down the hall.

She's old.

I mean ancient.

Like Jesus old or maybe even older. Who's older than Jesus? God, I suppose.

She's God old.

Her white hair is tied up on top of her head in a loose knot, and there are so many wrinkles on her face, there isn't any part of her that's smooth. The wrinkles are so deep and twisty, each one is like a road map to all the different stories of her life. She has on a flowery dress and bright pink lipstick that looks like it's slipping off where it's supposed to be. And her eyes are the deepest blue I've ever seen, like the sky on a really clear day when there isn't one single cloud.

"Come in. Come in." She smiles a big smile that makes her eyes disappear in all those wrinkles.

Tobin pulls the screen door open. She leans down and wraps her thick arms around him. His arms don't make it all the way around her.

"Mrs. Dickerson, I'd like you to meet my new assistant, Lemonade Liberty Witt." Tobin points a thumb in my direction. "Lemonade, this is Mrs. Dickerson. She used to teach third grade at Willow Creek Elementary before she retired."

She smiles at me and holds out a hand for me to shake.

"Hello there, it's so nice to meet you, Lemonade."

"I ate a bug," I blurt out.

She looks surprised and then smiles even bigger, her blue eyes disappearing again.

"Oh, well, that can happen now and again. Nothing to worry about, though, I'm sure. Well, Lemonade, I heard you were coming in to stay with Charlie. I'm so sorry to hear about Elizabeth, dear. Such a tragedy . . . and so young, too."

I look down at the smeared spot on my shoe and swallow the lump that always finds its way up my throat when someone says her name.

*Elizabeth Lilly Witt.*

Tobin stares back and forth between us, shifting his feet.

"I remember her very well," Mrs. Dickerson goes on.

"My mom?" I look back up at her, studying her wrinkles again and wondering which ones might hold stories about Mama. "You know her?"

"Oh, goodness' sakes, yes. She was in my class one year and was also very good friends with my youngest girl, Violet."

It feels weird to hear about Mama this way. It's like I thought I knew her better than anyone in the whole entire world, and now I find out I didn't know lots of things about her.

"You look just like her at that age." Mrs. Dickerson smiles again.

I can't help but smile now too.

"I do?"

"Oh, my, yes." She laughs a little. "And you know what? She was unique."

"Unique?"

"Yes, very much so. Quite an individual," Mrs. Dickerson goes on. "I remember when she was right around your age and she got a doctor kit for Christmas. Well, don't you know she opened up her very own free clinic for all the animals in town? She made house calls too, for the horses and steers. What did she call it?"

"She did that?" I ask. "Well, she loves animals, you know. She's a veterinarian back home."

Mrs. Dickerson smiles like she already knows.

"What did she call it?" she says again. "Well, anyway, I remember she loved learning anything she could about animals. She checked out every book we had up at the school library on all kinds of different species. From cats and dogs to horses and livestock. And she was busy at her clinic too. Many people brought their small animals to Charlie's garage to see her, and of course also to visit with Charlie and Rebecca. What was the name of it? It was such a unique name."

Tobin is a bubbling pot ready to explode, shifting his feet faster now and still looking back and forth between Mrs. Dickerson and me.

Mrs. Dickerson looks at me for a long time, like she's mulling me over.

"You're the spitting image of your mother, Lemonade Liberty Witt," she finally says. "That's certainly a one-of-a-kind name, isn't it? Although I wouldn't expect anything different from Elizabeth."

"Everyone just calls me Lem," I say.

"Ah, well." She places a warm hand on my shoulder. "Welcome to Willow Creek, Lem. I'm looking forward to getting to know you— *The Rainbow Bunny Animal Hospital and More!*" Mrs. Dickerson blurts out. "That's what it was. Thank the stars, I would have been up all night trying to remember—"

That's when Tobin lets out the biggest sigh you've ever heard.

"Ah . . . Mrs. Dickerson?" He finally bubbles over. "Can you show us where you saw the Bigfoot now?"

# 8

# DERMAL RIDGES

"I'm sure there are fingerprints to dust for this time," Mrs. Dickerson tells us, sliding her cane toward the kitchen in the back of the house.

The whole place smells like sugar and cinnamon and nutmeg and peanut butter and fresh-brewed tea leaves. It makes my stomach moan.

"I was in the kitchen here, baking, and wasn't I surprised to turn around and see a Bigfoot staring at me through the window, of all things! Leaned up right there on the sill." She nods to the window facing the thick woods out back. "When I turned to look at him, he growled at me through the glass. Right here is where I dropped the hot pan of cookies I had just taken out of the oven." She motions to a small indentation in the wood floor.

Tobin aims his Polaroid camera at the dent and takes

a picture of it. The camera spits out a photo. He grabs the photo and hands it to me.

"Exhibit A," he says, and turns back to Mrs. Dickerson. "Then what happened?"

"Well, I had to throw all those cookies in the trash, of course."

"No, Mrs. Dickerson, with the Bigfoot," Tobin says.

"Oh, yes, well, the pan had made this horribly loud bang, which must have startled him, because that's when he darted off into the trees. But not before giving the loudest, shrillest scream I've ever heard in all my days. It made the hairs on the back of my neck stand straight up. My goodness, it was something, all right."

"We can check for prints on the glass and the sill," Tobin tells me, adjusting his chin strap. "I sure hope you're right this time, Mrs. Dickerson."

"You know I keep my camera here just in case, but it happened so quickly I didn't get the chance to grab it." Mrs. Dickerson points to the camera hanging on a hook next to the refrigerator.

"Me and my assistant will go check out the window in question, then bring all the evidence back to HQ to further evaluate it." Tobin nods at me all official-like.

"HQ?" I roll my eyes, then head out the back door and down the cement steps with Tobin at my heels.

"That's right, Headquarters," he says, and then points to the ground just under the kitchen window and takes a picture of it. "Grass. No footprints to cast."

I watch him take off his glasses and eyeball every inch of

the window, his nose so close that his breath makes small circles of fog on the panes. Then he carefully sets his leather case on the ground and unzips it. He pulls out a jar filled with blackish powder and also a big round paintbrush. I watch him swirl the brush inside the jar of powder and then brush in tiny circles along the window and windowsill. The powder smears into a messy grayish cloud all over the glass.

"I don't think she's going to like you doing that to her window," I tell him.

"This is how you dust for prints," he says, pushing up his glasses with his forearm. "No footprints to cast, but there could be finger- or palm prints on the window."

"Bigfoot *fingerprints*?"

He sighs like I'm the biggest dope in the entire universe.

"The Bigfoot is a descendant of Gigantopithecus," he explains as he swirls the brush. "It's a species of giant ape from Asia that is believed to have been extinct for more than a million years. What we know is that humans have friction skin, like fingerprints, or dermal ridges, that usually go in one direction, and primates have dermal ridges that usually go in another. Plus, they're coarser and wider. I'm dusting to see what types of prints these are. Human or nonhuman prints."

"Oh . . ." is all I can think of to say. "What do you want me to do?"

"Grab the tape from the case, and we'll see if we can lift some prints from the glass."

I bend down and dig through his leather case. There's a movie camera inside, a bunch of packets of unused film, extra pens, tweezers, and one silver dollar. At the bottom I feel something else and pull it out. It's an old picture of some man with reddish-brown curls, leaned up against a silver convertible and holding a baby.

"Who's this?" I hold up the picture.

Tobin doesn't even hear me. Now he's examining his grayish, cloudy masterpiece with a magnifying glass that he's pulled out of his back pocket.

"Who's this?" I ask again.

Tobin turns to look at what I'm holding in my hand and then turns back toward the window.

"My dad," he says.

"Is that you with him?" I ask him.

He sighs one of those loud sighs again.

"Did you find the tape or not?"

"Sorry," I say, putting the picture back in and digging down deeper to find a roll of Scotch tape.

"I don't have a dad," I say matter-of-factly, holding out the tape in his direction.

"What do you mean you don't have a dad?" he asks without taking his eyes off the glass. "Everyone has a dad."

"Not me," I say. "Mama told me he didn't want to be a father when I was born. So I guess you could say that technically I don't have one. Here—"

He looks at me.

"The tape." I hold it toward him.

"Don't need it," he sighs. "There are no prints to lift."

"So you don't need the tape?"

"Mrs. Dickerson." Tobin motions through the glass. "I'm just not seeing anything come up back here."

She pokes her head out the back screen door. "Well . . . isn't that a shame? Are you absolutely sure?"

"Pretty sure." He examines the window again through the magnifying glass. "I'm not finding a fingerprint or a palm print or anything."

"Well, fiddlesticks!" She looks disappointed.

Tobin shakes his head and drops his hands to his sides.

"Nope, there's just nothing," he says, looking back up at her in the doorway.

"My goodness, I hate to have you kids come all this way out for nothing. How about some cookies and tea before you leave? I have peanut butter and molasses fresh out of the oven this morning," she says, her wrinkles swallowing up her eyes.

# 9

# SOUR LEMONS

At dinner that night I stare at my plate with my arms crossed over my chest.

Turns out Charlie is quite the gourmet.

Boiled hot dogs à la Wonder Bread with one squirt of ketchup and one squirt of mustard and a pile of Tater Tots on the side that are still cold in the middle.

Tobin and Charlie are working on a thousand-piece puzzle at the kitchen table while they eat. It's a basket of kittens playing with two blue yarn balls. Right now, Tobin and Charlie are searching for corner and edge pieces.

"Mama always makes greens with dinner," I inform Charlie.

"Mmmm-hmmm," Charlie says, examining a puzzle piece from behind his glasses. "Tell me what you kids have been up to today."

"I made Lemonade my assistant and then we went over to Mrs. Dickerson's again. This time she saw one peeking in the window, so we went out to dust for prints," Tobin tells him with his mouth full of boiled Oscar Mayer. "But we didn't get anything this time either, even though she swears she saw one."

"Mmmm," Charlie says. "This a corner?"

Tobin squints at it.

"Nope."

Charlie puts it back on the table.

"She made her famous peanut butter cookies, so it was still worth the trip, right?" Tobin looks at me. "Oh, and she told all kinds of stories about Lemonade's mom. She was best friends with Mrs. Dickerson's daughter Violet. Did you know that?" Tobin asks Charlie.

"Mmmm-hmmm," Charlie says, holding up another piece. "Here's a straight edge."

"Yep," Tobin agrees. "I didn't know she had nine children."

"Ah . . . nine? Yeah, that sounds right," Charlie says. "Don't ask me to name them all, though, I couldn't do it."

Tobin looks at me again.

"Oh, and . . . this one ate a bug." He points his head in my direction and snickers behind his hand. "It's all she's talked about all day."

"What are you laughing at?" I snap.

He stops.

"It's not funny at all," I say. "That thing might be laying eggs inside my stomach as we speak, and I could die any second from an insect-related scourge infesting my intestines."

"See what I mean?" Tobin says to Charlie. "You can't die

from swallowing a bug, can you, Charlie? I already told her, but she doesn't believe me."

"I can't say I've ever heard of anyone perishing from swallowing a bug, no," Charlie says, examining another puzzle piece.

I push my plate away and stand up.

"Well, maybe you both don't know everything. Ever think of that?" I put my hands on my hips. "Maybe they'll write about me in the medical journals because I'll be the very first!"

Tobin dips a Tot in a puddle of ketchup and takes a bite. There's ketchup on the side of his mouth, and he doesn't even lick it off. He's too busy examining me like I'm one of his stupid puzzle pieces. Trying to figure out what shape I am and where I fit.

"You know, you sure complain a lot," he says, chewing and staring just like the vile-smelling cows out in the pastures.

He can't be talking to me. Not *me*. He thinks he knows exactly what shape I am, and he doesn't know anything. I'm not a corner or an edge piece.

I'm me.

Lemonade Liberty Witt.

I want to tell them both that I don't belong here. Not on an edge or in a corner, or even anywhere in the middle.

"That's not so!" I tell him. "You don't even know me!"

"I know you complain a lot."

"You better take that back!" I warn him. "Charlie, tell him to take that back!"

Charlie looks up then, slowly removing his glasses and

leaning way back in his chair. He begins to examine me just like Tobin.

"My mom always says I can take any lemons that life gives me and make lemonade. That's why she named me Lemonade. Because that's what she does, and that's what I do too," I inform them both. "I'm the spitting image of her. Mrs. Dickerson even said so."

"Well, you sure don't seem to be very good at it." Tobin pops another sloppy red Tot into his mouth.

I feel tears prickling in my eyes.

"How would you even know, anyway? I have a million friends in the city and they all know that about me—"

"Hey." Tobin turns to Charlie. "Maybe that's why they call her Lem instead of Lemonade. 'Cause the lemonade she makes isn't lemonade at all, it's all sour and tart, and instead of sugar, she adds a whole lot of bellyaching."

My eyes want to cry.

My mouth wants to scream.

My fists want to punch him in his stupid safari hat still strapped tight under his chin.

"Well, you know what, Tobin Sky?" I holler at him. "You can just go and suck a lemon."

I turn and stomp down the hall.

"Why in Sam Hill would I want to suck a lemon?" Tobin is saying.

Charlie takes a deep breath and sighs out real long, like a deflated balloon.

"Give her some time," I hear him say. "She's had some really big lemons to deal with lately. Sometimes it takes a while to figure out just how to get the sweetest juice when they're bigger than you expect. Bigger than what's even fair. You of all people should understand that."

"Are we still talking about the girl or are we talking about the drink?" Tobin asks.

I grab the tarnished brass knob on the second door on the right, ready to give it a good, loud slam, when all the happy family pictures hanging on the wall of the hallway catch my eye.

A mom.

A dad.

And a girl.

One at the beach, another one skiing in the mountains, and even one on a ferryboat ride under the Golden Gate Bridge.

There's a picture in a round frame of just the redheaded girl on a hill, sitting in long green grass. She's squinting in the sun. She has a single red braid down her back, tied at the end with an orange and green crocheted yarn braid. Freckles are sprinkled across her face, her arms, and her legs. She's waving to the camera and smiling a big goofy grin. I lift the picture off the hook and inspect it more closely.

She's as bright as the sunshine washing over her. She's bubbling over and brimming with zest.

She *is* lemonade.

And I am too. The spitting image. Mrs. Dickerson even said so.

Except that I don't feel sunny or bubbly or zesty. I feel like a volcano ready to spew lava in every direction.

There isn't anything Lemonade about that.

Maybe Tobin was right. Maybe I've forgotten how to be me. Maybe I'll never be me again. Maybe I won't ever make lemonade for the rest of my entire life.

I stare at the happy girl in the grass until all the tears filling my eyes blur the picture.

# 10

# YOU ARE MY SUNSHINE

My all-time favorite sundae is vanilla ice cream with a glob of Marshmallow Fluff, a spattering of rainbow sprinkles on the side, and a mix of exactly fifty percent hot fudge and fifty percent caramel. Mama's is chocolate ice cream with chunks of banana, whipped cream, and a cherry on top. She doesn't care as much about ratios.

Our all-time favorite place to go in the city for sundaes is Sunshine's on the Bay. That's where we are today, sitting at their very best table. It's the one next to the front window that looks out over the water. From that spot we can watch all the sailboats and ships going back and forth across the bay. We can even hear the barking sea lions sunning themselves on the docks outside.

Today is perfect.

Sunny and warm and perfect.

On perfect days like this, every table at Sunshine's is full. And today is no different. Mama and I have on our best sundresses and our fancy sandals with the gold buckles on the heels. She's telling me all about the free animal clinic she opened up in Charlie's garage and all the animals that came to see her.

Someone knocks loud on the front window.

Bang. Bang. Bang.

"Lemonade!"

Bang. Bang. Bang.

"Lemonade Liberty Witt!"

I turn to see Tobin Sky, Willow Creek's official Bigfoot detective. He's standing on the sidewalk wearing his Bigfoot safari hat strapped tight under his chin, with his Polaroid hanging from his neck. He's peering at me between cupped hands through the front window. Painted letters on the glass advertise the ice cream of the month.

Suck a Lemon Sundae Supreme.

"Lemonade!" he calls again. "We got another call!"

"Mama, this is Tobin . . . ," I say, turning back to face her.

But the chair across from me is empty.

"Mama?" I call, looking around the shop.

But now the place is empty and everyone is gone. Even Mr. Bingham at the counter, who wears a paper hat and always gives me extra sprinkles.

"Lemonade!"

Bang. Bang. Bang.

My eyes peel open. I stare straight up at a star-free ceiling, which hangs above a bare-naked wood floor. An itchy wool blanket covers me, and the round frame of the redheaded girl's picture is lying next to me on the bed.

Bang. Bang. Bang.

I pull myself up and drag my tired body to the window. I feel all worn out, and my eyes are hot and scratchy. When I push the faded blue curtains to one side, Tobin is standing there staring at me from under his safari hat.

"What do you want?" I holler back at him through the glass, rubbing at my eyes.

"Employees at Bigfoot Detectives Inc. clock in at precisely oh eight-thirty hours," he tells me.

"What time is it?"

"It's oh eight-thirty-five hours." He holds his watch up to show me. It has a smiling cartoon Bigfoot on it with hairy brown arms that are pointing to an eight and a seven.

"And we just got another call." He waves the yellow legal pad at me.

I push the window up.

"Mrs. Dickerson again?" I ask, thinking that fresh molasses cookies sound like a way better breakfast than sticks and seeds and bark.

"No, the Millers out on Miller Ranch had an encounter. They think they caught something on film during a hunting trip. They have pictures. Hurry and get dressed."

"Can't," I inform him. "I'm calling in sick today."

"Sick?" He puts his hands on his hips. "You can't call in sick on your second day of work."

"Says who?"

"Section two, article five of the Bigfoot Detectives Employee Manual," he says.

"How do you have an employee manual for a business without any employees?"

"I typed it up last night," he says. "And article five, paragraph six, specifically addresses tardiness, attendance, and professional demeanor."

I yawn and rub at my eyes again.

"And I have to tell you, this doesn't look good under any of those categories," he goes on.

"Fine," I say. "I'll meet you in the garage."

"You mean the Bigfoot Headquarters."

"Yeah, right. *HQ.*"

"When?"

"I don't know," I say, exasperated. "Five or ten minutes."

"Well, which is it? Five or ten?"

"Five, okay? Five minutes."

He checks his watch, pushes a few buttons, winds it, and then lifts it up to his ear.

"I will expect to see you at the Bigfoot Detectives Headquarters at oh eight-forty-two hours, then," he says. "Do you want to synchronize?"

I roll my eyes and slam the window shut.

# 11

# A WAD OF ELMER'S GLUE
# AND A VERY WRONG NUMBER

After I yank on a pair of jean shorts and pull a San Francisco T-shirt over my head, I carefully twist my red curls into one long braid down my back. I pull Mama's suitcase out from under the bed and untie the orange and green crocheted yarn braid on the handle.

"Elizabeth Lilly Witt," I whisper, touching the letters of Mama's writing.

It's an important name. The most important name in the whole universe. I say it out loud every day so the universe remembers how important it is, and that it still matters to someone.

And also so it doesn't disappear.

Like she did.

I slide the name tag under my pillow and tie the yarn at the end of my braid, just like the zesty girl in the picture.

I check myself in the mirror above the sink in the bathroom.

The spitting image. Mrs. Dickerson said so.

I grab my shoes from the front hall and sit on the floor to tie them. That's when my eye catches something new on the kitchen counter and I stretch my neck to get a better look.

On the counter, next to the toaster, is a ten-pack of Twinkies.

* * *

Tobin is sitting at the ratty desk shuffling through his yellow legal pad when I make it to the Bigfoot Headquarters.

"You're late," he says flatly, looking at his Bigfoot watch and then at me. "It's now oh eight-fifty-three hours. I'll let you off with a warning this time, but if it happens again, I'm going to have to make a note of it in your employee file."

"You do that," I tell him, stuffing the last of my breakfast Twinkie in my mouth.

Tobin stares at me.

"*That's* what you're having for breakfast?"

"Yep," I say with my mouth full.

"I don't think Charlie would think that's very nutritious."

"S'pose not," I say, sucking the filling off the plastic wrapper.

Tobin wrinkles up his nose and watches me as I lick.

"You . . . ah, you have whipped cream on your chin." He points.

While I'm wiping my mouth with my arm, the green phone jingles. Tobin dives to grab it before it has a chance to ring again.

"Hello? Bigfoot Detectives Inc. We provide a full range of Bigfoot services for your convenience. How may we help you today?"

Tobin listens for a minute. I watch his eyebrows come together and his cheeks turn bright pink. Then he slams the phone down without saying one word.

I jump.

He sits frozen while I wait for him to say something. But he doesn't.

"Who *was* that?" I finally ask.

He tucks his yellow legal pad under his arm and stands up.

"Wrong number," he says.

"What did they say?"

"Nothing." He grabs his leather case. "Let's go, it'll take a good twenty minutes to get out to the Miller Ranch by bike. They got some pictures developed and think maybe they got something on film."

"Okay," I say.

Tobin stops in front of me and holds his hand out. There's something in it.

"Here," he says.

In his palm is a handmade name badge with a carefully printed name on the front.

### LEMONADE LIBERTY WITT
*Assistant Bigfoot Detective*

On the back there's a safety pin stuck in a wad of clumped-up Elmer's. It makes me feel kind of important to see my name in writing like that. Especially with the title and all.

"Thanks," I tell him, taking it.

"Yeah, well, you pledged the oath and all, so we needed to make it official."

The rims around his eyes are redder than normal, and I wonder if it has anything to do with that wrong number.

"So, when do I get my hat?" I ask, pinning the badge to the front of my T-shirt.

"A *hat*? Oh, no, you can't get a hat until you make partner," he tells me. "A hat is a much higher level of security clearance. You'd have to take a whole different oath and everything. Nope, we're nowhere near a hat."

"Why not?"

"Those are the rules."

"Whose rules?"

"Official corporation rules."

"What if I make my own hat?"

"No, no, no." He shakes his head. "Nope, that wouldn't be right. It wouldn't be official. Uh-uh . . . it's only for partners in the Inc. You said you don't want to be a partner, right? 'Cause you aren't staying. That's what you said, right?"

"Yep," I say. "That's right. I'm blowing this Popsicle stand."

"You just ate a Twinkie."

"What? No, I mean yes, I'm leaving," I say, straightening my new badge. "Definitely leaving."

"Then all you get is that." He points to my front.

"Fine."

The phone rings and Tobin turns to ice again.

Ring.

"Aren't you going to get that?" I ask.

"No," he says, heading toward the door. "We have to go, and you already made us late enough."

"What if it's another sighting?" I ask. "What if it's *the* sighting? What if it's Mrs. Dickerson with warm cookies fresh from the oven?"

"It's not. Plus, the machine can get it. Hurry up." Tobin puts a hand on the knob.

Ring.

I lunge toward the desk and grab the receiver.

"Don't!" he hollers.

"Hello?" I say. "Bigfoot Detectives Inc. We can . . . ah, handle Bigfoot things . . . or sightings and . . . ah, look for dental ridges and, yeah, whatever needs Bigfoot-related . . . ah, needs that you feel are . . . um . . . hello?"

Tobin hits his forehead with his palm and shakes his head at me.

"Dermal ridges," he whispers. "Dermal ridges, not dental."

"Help me!" a voice screeches in my ear. "Bigfoot is eating me!"

"What?" I ask.

Laughter.

"Who is this?" I demand.

"Tobin, help save me from the Bigfeet!" the voice screeches again.

More laughing.

I can feel my volcano bubbling up and over the sides, ready to spurt smoldering-hot lava up to the sky. I look at Tobin, and he turns away.

"It's Big*FOOT*, you stupid idiot!" I tell the kid on the other end of the line. "Big*FOOT*! It's not plural. It's singular. *Singular!* Everyone who's anyone knows that!"

The receiver on the other end slams down with a bang.

Tobin's back is to me now, his hand still on the doorknob.

"Wrong number?" he asks without turning around.

I slip the phone receiver back into its cradle.

"Yeah," I say. "Definitely a wrong number."

He stands there a few more seconds without looking at me, and then pushes the door open without saying one word.

# 12

# BIGFOOT SOUVENIRS AND MORE

Mr. Miller's son, Jay, shows us four pictures that are blurry at best.

Grainy at least.

And just plain dark and fuzzy.

Tobin tells him that anything is better than nothing. But after seeing these pictures, I think this anything is a real close second to nothing. I guess whatever's in the pictures could be something if you squint your eyes real tight and cock your head to the left. And we know for sure it's not a tree stump or anything like that, because in each picture it's in a different spot and a different position.

But is it a Bigfoot?

Tobin makes an executive decision to bring in an expert witness to give the final yea or nay about the images in the grainy shots, so we stop in at Charlie's store that afternoon.

The store is set on the edge of Highway 299 and made entirely of logs. Even the roof is made of thick, heavy logs. The store has a dark green wooden door with a bell on it, so that whenever someone opens it, the thing jingles to let Charlie know there's a new customer.

The bell on the door rings when Tobin and I push it open, which makes Charlie look up at us from behind the counter where he's sitting on a stool reading a book. Right next to the door is a big bulletin board with newspaper clippings of Bigfoot sightings. Some from California and others from other states. There's even an article about a Bigfoot story someone told President Theodore Roosevelt in the 1800s.

"Well, there they are!" Charlie calls out, setting his book aside and taking off his glasses.

Tobin, the Millers' pictures in hand, makes a beeline for Charlie while I explore the shop. It's bigger on the inside than it looks on the outside, and there's a humongous stone fireplace right in the middle of the room with fat, lumpy pillows scattered across the floor all around. There's a hand-carved sign over the fireplace that says:

## TAKE A STORY, LEAVE A STORY

In the far corner is a gargantuan wooden Bigfoot, a little like the one at the center of town. Except this Bigfoot is holding another carved sign, letting customers know that they can get their picture taken with it for a dollar.

The shelves are covered in anything and everything Bigfoot-related—posters, greeting cards, T-shirts, coffee mugs, and even a Bigfoot doormat, which is just one big brown foot.

There are other sections too, all clearly labeled with even more carved wooden signs. In the FINE CUISINE section there is an aisle labeled EXOTIC JERKIES OF THE WORLD. There is any kind of jerky a person could ever want.

If you're a person who eats the stuff, that is. Which I'm not. Beef, deer, bear, elk, buffalo, ostrich, and even kangaroo.

Disgusting.

Next to the jerkies are jars of olives stuffed with things like garlic and nuts and cheese. There are all kinds of fancy crackers with seeds on them and some cookies, too.

There is a section labeled HUNTING AND FISHING, which is where I see a whole basket of safari hats, just like the one Tobin wears. Except these are all plain with no letters on them. I pick one up.

"Tobin," I call, modeling it for him. "What do you think?"

"Nope," he tells me. "I already told you. You're not approved for that level of security clearance. Come on, now, we have to show Charlie the pictures."

I walk up to the counter and rest my elbows on the glass. There's a spinning tower of Bigfoot key chains, a box of maps, and a basket of saltwater taffy, each piece individually wrapped in wax paper.

Two for a nickel.

"What do you think?" Charlie asks after I've thoroughly examined the place. He picks out a pink piece of taffy for me and hands Tobin a brown one.

"It really is Bigfoot Souvenirs and More," I tell him, unwrapping the taffy and putting it in my mouth.

"S'pose so." He smiles at me.

I turn away.

"Charlie," Tobin says, pushing up his glasses. "When did the Fotomat say the film is going to be developed?"

"They said four days," Charlie says. "So maybe Thursday. You kids had your lunch yet?"

"Not yet," Tobin tells him, and juts his chin in my direction. "This one had a Twinkie for breakfast."

Big fat blabbermouth.

"We can call Diesel's Deli and have them make us up some sandwiches. How does that sound?"

"Can you look at these first?" Tobin asks Charlie, handing him the envelope of pictures.

The bell on the door dings. We all look up to see a family. A mom, a dad, and a little girl about four years old.

"Welcome!" Charlie calls out to them, slowly getting up from his stool. "Welcome to Bigfoot Souvenirs and More! We have everything and anything related to the elusive Bigfoot that you could ever want to take home with you! Please let me know if I can help you find anything."

"Thank you," the man says, while the girl runs to the section labeled TOYS, which is filled with baskets of stuffed Bigfoot and other animals of the forest.

"Okay." Charlie settles back down on his stool and pulls his glasses out of his shirt pocket. "Let's see what you got here."

While Charlie and Tobin lay the four pictures out on the

counter, I watch the man and the woman and the girl go through the stuffed toys. They smile and laugh together. I bet somewhere they have a happy house with a happy hallway full of happy family pictures.

And I bet one day soon there will be another one showing their happy trip to Willow Creek.

I sigh.

"We just got back from a call out at the Miller Ranch," Tobin is telling Charlie. "Mr. Miller and his son Jay got these while they were out hunting. We're wondering what you think about them."

Tobin lines up the four pictures in perfect order in front of Charlie.

"They're blurry," Tobin tells him.

"And grainy," I say.

"Mmmm-hmmm," Charlie says, leaning over the pictures.

We all examine them together. Tobin pulls his magnifying glass from his back pocket to get a closer look. He lets me and Charlie take turns too.

"Well," Charlie says, stroking his beard. "Whatever it is, it's definitely big, isn't it?"

"Bipedal, too," Tobin says.

"What's that?" I ask.

"*Bipedal* means it walks on two feet," Tobin explains.

"Don't bears do that too?" I ask.

"Very good, Lem," Charlie says. "You're exactly right. But there are some big differences in determining whether it's a bear or a Bigfoot."

"Like what?"

"Well, Bigfoot has longer hair, and it's scraggly, too. It's been mostly reported as reddish brown. Kind of like an orangutan. But sometimes it's reported in other colors. Some black, some dark brown—"

"Some even gray," Tobin adds.

"That's right," Charlie says. "And they smell real strong, too, like a skunk. They're bipedal creatures all the time, just like humans, whereas bears generally walk on all fours and only sometimes stand up on their hind legs."

"And Bigfoot has the facial features of a human." Tobin looks at me, his wire-rims slipped all the way down to the tip of his nose. "Half human, half primate."

"And opposable thumbs like us." Charlie wiggles his thumbs. "Instead of paws like bears."

I look through the magnifying glass again. Real close this time, with my nose almost pressed against the picture.

"Ever think it could be someone in a suit, just trying to mess with you?" I ask.

"No!" Tobin blurts out. "See, there you go again! There she goes again!" He waves his arms at Charlie.

"What?" I say, confused. "What did I say?"

"Always with the complaining." Tobin begins gathering up the photos in a huff.

"I'm not complaining," I say, then turn to Charlie. "I'm not. I'm just asking a question. Could it be somebody in a suit? How can it be scientific if you don't consider every possibility?"

"Don't you think I would know the difference?" Tobin

snaps at me. "I'm a professional, you know. Read the sign."
He points to his stupid hat.

"I think anyone could be fooled if the conditions were right and it was far enough away. Plus, there's a big difference between seeing something in real life and looking at grainy pictures," I say. "But this is all you've got. Geez, why are you getting so upset?"

"She's right," Charlie tells Tobin. "We have to ask all kinds of questions and not just assume. And yes, Lem, to answer your question, some have doubted the original film that Roger Patterson and Bob Gimlin shot out this way. Asking the same question. Could it be a fake? Could they or someone else have fooled us all with a costume of some sort?"

"Do you think they did that?"

"No!" Tobin snaps again. "It's real. I know it. Charlie knows it too. He's even seen one with his own eyes. Tell her, Charlie. Tell her they're real."

I turn to Charlie.

For a minute I wonder if Mama ever saw a Bigfoot. She never talked about it, but I'm finding out a lot of things about Mama here that I never knew about.

"You've actually *seen* one?" I ask Charlie.

Charlie sighs a long breath and puts his glasses in his shirt pocket. "That's right." He leans back on his stool, crossing his arms over his chest.

"When?"

"It was one night about five years ago now. I was driving out on this highway here. It was dark and foggy with just a bit of drizzle coming down, which means all I could see was the few feet in front of the car that my headlights lit up. I was driving real slow . . . real slow. And then in a flash of a second he was there. Right there in front of me."

"Really?" I breathe.

"Yes, really," Tobin says. "Let him tell the story, why don't you?"

"The first thing I saw was the eye shine," Charlie goes on. "Bright red eye shine gleaming in my headlights. And then he was standing there."

"Out in front of the car?"

"That's right," Tobin interrupts again. "Nothing hullabaloo about that, is there?"

I turn back to Charlie. "Did you hit him?"

Charlie swallows and shakes his head slowly.

"No, thank God. I stomped my boot on the brake pedal, fast as I could. He stood there staring at me through the windshield, and I couldn't move. It was like he put a spell on me or something." Charlie stares off into the distance. "We just sat a moment, looking at each other. Like neither of us knew what to do."

"Then what happened?" I ask.

"Then . . . he was gone. As fast as he came." Charlie puts his chin in his hand and leans an elbow on the counter. "At first, I wondered if it could have been something else. *Anything* else. The fog was so thick . . ." Then Charlie looks right into me. "But I know it wasn't. It was a Bigfoot. A real live Bigfoot."

"Wow," I whisper. "Were you scared?"

Charlie doesn't say anything for a real long time, like he's thinking hard about my question.

"Funny thing is, I wasn't," he finally tells me. "We looked each other square in the eye for that split second, and I knew in that moment . . . he was more scared of me than I was of him."

"How could that be?" I ask. "The thing's a beast. A monster."

"Wrong again!" Tobin says, his voice quivering a little. "Just 'cause you don't understand them doesn't make them beasts or monsters!"

I put my hands on my hips and give him a long, hard glare.

"What is your problem?" I demand.

"Excuse me," the man calls from the back of the store, standing next to the big wooden Bigfoot statue. "Can we get a picture with the beast?"

Tobin just hits his forehead with his palm and shakes his head.

# 13

# FINALLY THURSDAY

"What time is it now?" Tobin asks, tapping his Bigfoot watch and holding it to his ear. He's sitting at Charlie's kitchen table finishing a blue yarn ball in the puzzle.

It's finally Thursday.

"Five minutes past the last time you asked me," I tell him, giving the boiling Oscar Mayers another good stir at the stove.

I didn't think Tobin was actually going to make it to this day. The day that the film from the Fotomat is supposed to be ready. He's only talked about it every single second of every single day.

"Didn't he say he was going to close a few minutes early to pick up the film from the Fotomat? Where is he already?" Tobin shakes his wrist this time, like that's going to make the Bigfoot arms move faster.

"He'll be here when he gets here. Check the Tater Tots. They should be light brown."

He ignores me while he searches for all the puzzle pieces with blue in them. I grab the quilted oven mitt myself.

"Did you hear that?" The kitchen chair scrapes on the floor, and he jumps up from the table, darting out of the room. The screen door slams.

I open the oven and pull out the pan of Tater Tots. They are a Tater Tot masterpiece, superbly browned with the perfect amount of crispness.

The screen door slams again.

"False alarm," Tobin announces, sitting back down and adjusting his chin strap.

I found out that he only takes the hat off for bed and baths. I also found out his mother is a nurse at St. Joseph's Hospital all the way in Blue Lake and only has Sundays off, which is why he's always at Charlie's house. I still don't know about his dad.

Tobin never talks about him.

"Where is he?" Tobin says, tapping his watch again.

"It's only five-fifteen," I tell him. "Didn't you two synchronize to seventeen hundred thirty-five hours?" I roll my eyes.

"Yeah."

"Well, it's not seventeen hundred thirty-five hours yet."

Which I also learned is really 5:35 in military time, but I only learned that because Tobin typed up a military time conversion chart for me.

Tobin sighs loudly and goes back to his puzzle. I pull three plates out of the cupboard and three forks from the drawer and fold three paper towels from the roll to set the table around him. At exactly 5:33, we hear Jake, Charlie's old station wagon, grumble up the driveway, and all I see is Tobin vapors and airborne puzzle pieces.

The screen door slams again.

"Did you get it? Did you get it?" Tobin demands from out on the front porch.

"Got it!" Charlie calls back to him. "Help me with this first."

I give the hot dogs one final stir in the pot, then turn the stove off and head out to meet them. When I get to the screen door, I see Charlie and Tobin pulling a bike out of the back end of Jake.

"What . . . what's that?" I ask, slowly pushing the door open.

Charlie carries the bike up the porch steps and sets it down in front of me.

"Can't get around on handlebars all summer," he tells me.

I stare at it.

It's beautiful. Possibly the most beautiful bike I've ever seen. The most beautiful bike that's ever been.

I point to myself. "It's for me?"

I can't stop staring at it. It's a light pink with a pink-and-green-striped banana seat and a brown wicker basket in the front. Perfect for the kitten Mama had promised me for my eleventh birthday.

I look up at Charlie. He's smiling real big. An actual, real smile with teeth and everything.

I smile back at him.

Then he nods like we've said all we need to say and pulls open the screen door, disappearing inside. Tobin comes up the steps, examining the movie roll over his wire-rims.

"Isn't it the most beautiful bike you've ever seen?" I breathe.

"What are you going on about a bike for when this is the moment that might go down in Bigfoot history? No! United States of America history! World history! This"—Tobin holds the film canister in my face and starts dancing a jig—"is it! Patterson, Gimlin, and Sky!" He sings as he dances. "Patterson, Gimlin, and Sky! Channel Four News, here I come!"

"What's the big deal with being on the news?" I ask.

"Because it means something if it's on the news. It's significant. It's important. It *matters*, and everyone will know it. Everyone will know me and know that I matter too. Me, Tobin Sky."

"Who says you don't matter now?" I ask him.

He stops dancing and stares at me.

"Hey," Charlie calls from inside. "What smells so good in here?"

• • •

Charlie eats three hot dogs with two helpings of Tater Tots. I eat two hot dogs with three helpings of Tater Tots. Tobin takes one bite of his hot dog and doesn't make a dent in his Tots, and then complains the whole time that we're the world's slowest eaters.

"I can't believe we're just sitting here eating boiled hot

dogs when cryptozoological history is about to be made," he gripes. "When are we going to watch the movie already?"

"How can you blame me for savoring my food when these gourmet hot dogs and Tots are the best I've had?" Charlie says to me. "What's your secret?"

"Well." I wipe my mouth with the paper towel. "I stir the hot dogs *while* they boil."

"Ahh!" He leans back in his chair. "Well, you've got the touch, there's no denying that."

I reach for another spoonful of Tots. Tobin puts his hand on top of mine.

"You've got to be kidding," he says.

"Okay," Charlie says, pushing his chair back from the table. "Let's get that movie laced up."

"Finally!" Tobin jumps up from his seat like a jack-in-the-box and runs out of the room.

● ● ●

Five minutes later, Charlie is sitting on a kitchen chair squinting through his glasses in front of the projector, trying to thread the film, while Tobin stands over him, giving him directions.

"In through there, yep . . . that's right, now in that way . . . right there . . . yep." Tobin points.

"I think he probably already knows how to do it," I say.

Tobin doesn't even hear me.

"Up that way, uh-huh," he goes on.

The projector kind of looks like an upside-down bicycle with two wheels. The film is wound up on the first wheel and snakes through tunnels and around knobs all through the machine until it comes out the back and winds up on the empty rear reel.

When they're finally ready, Tobin and I settle in on the living room sofa, which is covered in a big green leafy pattern, while Charlie closes the matching drapes over the front window.

"Ladies and gentlemen," Charlie announces. "Thank you for attending the Bigfoot Detectives first official Bigfoot screening. Is everyone ready to make history?"

"Ready!" we call back at the same time.

"Lights!"

He flicks the switch on the wall.

"Camera!"

The projector starts to clickity-clack as it pulls the movie through its tunnels and around its knobs.

"Action!" Tobin yells.

We wait, watching the wall in front of us where the light of the projector shines. First there are only gray squiggly lines bouncing, then a white square, and then a countdown. Five. Four. Three. Two. One.

Then the first image pops up.

It's a blurry forest.

A jumping blurry forest.

It feels a little like being on Tobin's handlebars with one eye closed in the dark. There are grainy trees, fuzzy bushes, and shadowy shapes. Tobin moves to the very edge of the couch, leaning closer to the images that bump and bumble against the wall.

"I'm running here," he explains. "That's why it's so jumpy."

"You can't see anything with you running like that," I tell him.

"Keep watching," he says, his eyes wide, searching every inch of each frame. "I stop when I get close to him."

After a while, it feels like I'm on a roller-coaster ride that's much too long, and I start to wish I hadn't eaten that last hot dog or that last helping of Tots.

"There!" Tobin points, bouncing up from his seat. "I saw him duck down there, behind that tree! That tree there! See it? Can you see him? He's right there."

Tobin's standing now, pointing to dark, hazy shapes bouncing against the wall.

"It's so dark," I say, leaning forward. "It looks like a tree stump to me."

"Are you blind? It's not a stump! He's there!" He points again. "Right between those two trees. Don't you see him?"

"Do you?" I ask.

He squints hard at the wall.

"Yes! He's there. Right there! Wait, no . . . he's there, right there! That dark shape behind this pine here. Wait . . ."

The projector chugs for a few more seconds. Then the film flies loose off the back reel, making a clicking sound. Charlie turns off the projector and flicks the light switch back on.

"I'm sorry, Tobin," Charlie says. "It was just too dark to say for sure what it was."

Tobin drops back down on the couch like a wet sack.

"Nothing." He sulks with his chin on his chest. "The Miller pictures were better than these."

I want to tell him, *"Look who's complaining now."*

I want to tell him, *"Look who doesn't know how to make lemonade now."*

But I don't.

"What we need to do is a real expedition." Tobin turns to me. "What do you say?"

"An expedition?" I ask.

"Yeah, we'll plan a camping trip out in the middle of the woods and stay there until we find something."

Did he say *the middle of the woods*? The woods where a real live woolly monster is supposedly living? Where there are bugs and snakes and bears and poison ivy and other generally disgusting and itchy and scary things?

When he talked expedition before, I guess I figured he meant a tent in Charlie's backyard. He didn't say anything about the woods.

Tobin is staring at me, waiting for my answer.

"I—I—"

I want to ask him where we'll sleep. What we'll eat. How we're supposed to go to the bathroom.

Instead, I think of the redheaded girl in the round frame hidden under my mattress.

The spitting image. Mrs. Dickerson said so. She's me, and I'm her. Somewhere inside me. Even if she's lost right now under molten lava that spews without warning.

"Ah . . . okay, I guess," I say.

*"Now how's that for making lemonade?"* I want to ask him.

But I don't.

Because I'm still worrying about where I'm going to go to the bathroom out in the middle of the woods.

# 14

# ALONE

"So, you're the famous Lemonade Liberty Witt that Tobin has been going on about," says Tobin's mom, sticking out a hand for me to shake.

I grab it. It's skinny with a big diamond ring on it. Her fingernails have sparkly pink polish on them.

"I'm Debbie Sky." She smiles at me.

She looks just like Tobin.

"Hello, Mrs.—" I start.

She stops me. "Oh, please, call me Debbie."

I try to smile back at her, but today my lips just don't feel like it.

Charlie and Debbie are sipping coffee on the yellow porch swing at Charlie's place. Tobin and I have just come back from investigating a new sighting at Mrs. Dickerson's.

Another false alarm.

Sunday is the only day that Charlie doesn't open the store and the only day that Debbie doesn't work her normal seven a.m. to seven p.m. shift at the hospital. And it's the only day that they have morning coffee on the big wrap-around porch.

She's pretty.

She has on faded Levi's with holes in the knees and a purple T-shirt. She has long blond curls tied up high in a ponytail, and she's wearing pale blue eye shadow and soft pink lipstick. She's barefoot, with the same sparkly pink polish on her toes that she has on her nails.

"It's so nice to meet you, Lemonade," she says. "I'm so sorry to hear about your mother, honey."

I look down at my feet and swallow away the lump.

"Mom," Tobin says. "Did you and Charlie decide about the expedition yet?"

"Tobin," Debbie says. "We are talking about something else right now." Then she turns to me again. "We were friends, you know. Me and your mom."

"No," I say, swallowing again. "I didn't know that."

"In high school. We worked together at Moon Shadow's, the ice cream shop in town . . . and went to see Elvis in concert in the city when we were eighteen . . ."

I think about Sunshine's on the Bay. Mama loved ice cream.

*Elizabeth Lilly Witt.*

"Unfortunately, we lost touch when she moved away," Debbie is saying.

Tobin is shifting his feet.

"Mrs. Dickerson said I should give these to you." I hold out the bag of cookies toward Charlie and Debbie.

"Oh, boy," Charlie says. "Her gingersnaps are the best in town."

"I had three of them," I tell him. "But I'm starting to wonder if she really sees anything at all, or if she just wants someone to make cookies for."

Charlie and Debbie look at each other but don't say anything.

"Today we went to investigate footprints in her vegetable garden, and there weren't any, were there?" I say to Tobin.

"Nothing," Tobin says.

"Mr. Dickerson died almost ten years ago now," Debbie says. "Isn't that right, Charlie?"

"Sounds about right, yeah," he answers, taking a cookie from the bag and dipping it in his black coffee.

"I imagine she gets real lonely in that house all by herself," Debbie says.

"Mrs. Dickerson had a husband who died?" I ask.

"That's right," Debbie tells me. "Oliver was his name. He was the principal of the school for many years."

*Oliver Dickerson.*

"*Mommm,*" Tobin bursts in. "What did you decide?"

"What, honey?"

"About the expedition," he says. "What did you decide?"

"Oh, right . . . Charlie?" Debbie motions in his direction and helps herself to a cookie from the bag.

"We decided you may plan an expedition—" Charlie starts, and then sips.

"Yes!" Tobin jumps up and down.

"Let me finish," Charlie says with one finger in the air. "We decided that you may plan an expedition; however, I will go with you."

"Even better!" Tobin starts jumping again.

"I will close the store up next weekend, and we can plan to leave for Bluff Creek Friday afternoon and return on Sunday."

"Sunday?" Tobin complains. "That's only two and a half days."

"Tobin," Debbie warns. "Charlie is being very generous to take this time off from the store."

"I know it, but *Sunday*?"

"Tobin." She gives him a stern look.

"Thank you, Charlie," Tobin says. "Actually, if we really get to go to Bluff Creek, two and a half days might be plenty of time to find something."

"So, we will plan on it, then," Charlie says.

"Isn't this the greatest, Lemonade? We're going to see a Bigfoot with our very own eyes!" Tobin exclaims. "Bluff Creek is where Patterson and Gimlin filmed their world-famous film. And where *we* will film *ours*."

I want to tell them all that I'd rather spend the weekend with Mrs. Dickerson instead of parading around the woods in the dark looking for a monster. Sipping tea, eating cookies, and hearing more stories about Mama sounds like a way better weekend to me.

But I can't say that. Tobin will tell me I'm just complaining again. The redheaded girl in the picture would go on an exciting expedition. Me too . . . before.

My lips used to want to smile, before.

They were happy.

*I* was happy.

Then everything changed.

I sit on the top step of the porch with my chin in my hand, watching Tobin and Charlie and Debbie chattering happily about the upcoming trip like nothing bad has ever happened. Like they don't have to hold something heavy everywhere they go.

Like they're carrying joy instead. Light, fluffy joy.

And even though I'm sitting right next to them, I feel all alone.

I try not to think of the day everything changed. The single worst day of my entire life. When Mama was in the hospital for the very last time. When she was too tired to open her eyes. And her fingers were too weak to curl around mine the way they always did. The day when I had to say good-bye . . . I don't want to think about it because when I do, the sadness pulls me in so deep sometimes it feels like I'll never find my way out.

"I'm going in to lie down," I tell Charlie.

"Oh . . . all right, Lem," he says. "You feeling okay?"

"Yeah," I say, forcing my lips to give him at least a half-grin. "Just tired, I guess."

I pull the screen door open and close it softly behind me. When I turn around, Charlie is still watching me through the screen.

# 15

# OPERATION:
# BLUFF CREEK EXPEDITION

". . . and number nine." Tobin sticks out his ninth finger. "The forest there is thick," he explains. "We know it's rich enough in resources to support a large omnivorous primate species. One that is rare and forages over a wide area . . . And finally, number ten, and this is the biggest reason Bluff Creek is the best place to find a Bigfoot . . . it's the place where Patterson and Gimlin shot the original film."

This is what I get when I make the mistake of asking Tobin a question about Bluff Creek. Yet another chapter of the *Bigfoot Encyclopaedia Britannica* spews from his lips.

It's Friday just after lunch, and we're on the driveway loading Jake up for the trip.

"It's not going to shut," I tell Charlie, shading my eyes from the sun.

He's been trying to close the back end of the station

wagon for the past fifteen minutes. It's packed with everything we'll need for our expedition in Bluff Creek. And then some. Three fat sleeping bag rolls, two days of food, pots, pans, clothes, jackets, towels, backpacks, a first aid kit, and one roll of toilet paper.

"I think we need a little teamwork," Charlie says. "On three?"

All three of us line our hands up along the back hatch.

"One, two, three," we all say together.

That does it. The door slams and the lock latches.

"Everybody ready?" Charlie asks.

"Ready!" Tobin hollers, scrambling into the front seat. "Shotgun!"

"It's all yours." I open the back door like I couldn't care less.

Which I couldn't.

Then we have to listen to Tobin flap his gums the whole way there. I surf wind waves with my hand out the window and do my best to ignore him. I have more important things to worry about at the moment.

First and foremost, where I'm going to go to the bathroom. And the more I think about having to go outside in the woods, the more I feel like I have to go right this minute. Even though the late-afternoon air is hot, and my back feels sticky against the tan vinyl, and my tongue is drier than dirt, I don't take even one sip of water from the canteen Charlie brought along.

"Hello? Earth to Lemonade," Tobin is saying.

"Huh?" I ask.

"Charlie's talking to you," he says.

"Oh . . . What?" I ask Charlie.

"I said I made it up to the elementary school yesterday morning to get you registered for the fall," Charlie says, looking at me in the rearview mirror.

I look away.

"Oh" is all I can think of to say to that.

Tobin turns around in the passenger seat to look at me.

"That mean you're staying?" He cracks a smile from under his safari hat.

"What's this?" Charlie asks.

"*Nothing*," I say, glaring at Tobin.

"Lemonade says she isn't staying," Tobin tells Charlie.

Big fat blabbermouth.

"She says that's the reason she can't be my partner. Because she's going home. What did you say? You're blowing this newsstand?"

"Wrong!" I say. "*You* said I couldn't be your partner. I didn't say I wouldn't be a partner. And it's a Popsicle stand, not a newsstand. Who blows a newsstand?"

"Who blows a Popsicle stand?" he asks. "And what does that even mean, anyway?"

He's got me there.

"And just so you know, I'm not making someone partner if they're going to just up and leave at any time."

Charlie's eyes are on me again in the rearview mirror. They have a lot of questions in them.

Questions I don't want to answer.

"Well, if your plans change," Charlie tells me, like he's

talking about the weather, "I've got you enrolled in the same fifth-grade class as Tobin with Mrs. Santamaria starting in September."

But the casual words that come out of his mouth don't match the eyes looking at me in the mirror.

"That's so cool!" Tobin flashes another smile at me. "She's the best teacher in fifth grade. She gives the least amount of homework and bakes cupcakes for the class when it's your birthday."

It's getting harder to breathe, and I can feel the volcano bubbling low in my gut. I want to tell them both not to count on me staying. I want to tell them both that I don't belong in this place. I want to tell them both that I'm going home.

But I don't.

Instead, for the rest of the trip, I pretend to be sleeping in the back while Tobin and Charlie play the license plate game, then the alphabet game, and then sing "Row, Row, Row Your Boat" about a zillion and one times.

First they just sing it regular, but then Tobin gets the idea to sing it in a round. Charlie couldn't carry a tune if his life depended on it, and he keeps starting in all the wrong places and adding all kinds of silly words instead of singing the right ones. Each time Charlie joins in, it gives Tobin a fit of giggles, and then they have to start all over again.

They sound like they're having fun, and it makes part of me wish I hadn't pretended to be sleeping the whole time. But I don't know how to invite myself in after I spewed my lava all over everything.

At just after six o'clock in the evening, we finally pull into the spot where we'll set up camp. Now I really have to go to the bathroom, and there isn't a single stall or outhouse or gas station in sight. I don't know how to ask Charlie about it, so I just hold it and shift my legs.

That works for a while, and then my gut starts hurting so bad, and the whole leg-shifting thing doesn't work anymore, and I think my bladder might explode. It makes me wonder if anyone has ever died from Explosive Bladder Syndrome.

Charlie and Tobin are still pounding stakes into the ground and setting up the tent while I'm unpacking the supplies. The last thing I pull out of a brown paper grocery bag is the roll of toilet paper. Which makes my bladder hurt even worse, and I decide I can't wait another second.

I tap Charlie on the arm.

"I . . . um . . . where do we . . . um—" I shift my legs and cross them under me.

"Ahhhh," Charlie says before I get any more words out. "Follow me. Tobin, we'll be right back."

I feel my cheeks burning. Tobin isn't even paying attention. He's too busy hammering at a stake.

Charlie grabs the roll of toilet paper and says, "Follow me. Bring the bag too. In the woods, we generally find a place and designate it the restroom area. Let's find one together where we can all have some privacy when we need it."

"You mean I really have to go in the middle of the woods?" I ask.

"That's right."

"What if a bear decides to make me his dinner while I'm out here going? Or a rattlesnake falls out of the trees and lands on my head and bites me in the nose? Or—"

"I promise you, it'll be fine. And I can stay with you, if you need me to."

"I'd rather be eaten," I mumble under my breath.

He chuckles.

I follow him through the woods until he finds a spot not real far from where Tobin's still hammering on the tent. It's a small clearing next to a fallen tree.

"Would you like me to stand over that way and wait for you?" Charlie asks me.

"Not even a little bit," I say, grabbing the toilet paper.

I want to tell him Mama buys double-ply. But I don't because my bladder isn't going to last till I get the words out.

"Okay, just right back up that same path we came down. Call out if you need me to come and get you. I'll hear you. You can just leave the roll of toilet paper there for everyone to use as they need."

"Okay, okay," I say, shifting from leg to leg.

I watch his dark blue Windbreaker through the trees and bushes until I can't see it anymore.

As if this day, this year, this life couldn't get any worse, now I'm unbuttoning my shorts, pulling down my Sears brand cotton underwear, and peeing in the woods.

At Mrs. Dickerson's, I'd be eating all the cookies I wanted and peeing in her flowery-smelling bathroom filled with lilac-colored rugs and towels that smell like Downy fabric softener. I bet she even has Mr. Bubble and a pink sponge, instead of just a stupid bar of Irish Spring and a plain blue washcloth.

# 16

# A TALKING LUMP OF WOOD

After the sun falls behind the trees and the woods grow dark and cool and even scarier, Charlie makes a roaring campfire. It lights our campsite with a warm, fiery glow that makes it feel like a safe, cozy living room out in the middle of nowhere.

On a griddle, he cooks up juicy hamburgers with slices of American cheese on top. Then he peels the label off the can of baked beans and places the can right near the flames to heat up. After I bite into my smoky, cheesy burger, I decide that Charlie can cook hamburgers in the woods way better than he can cook Oscar Mayers on the stove.

After supper, we roast marshmallows on long sticks we find in the woods. When the marshmallows are brown and crispy on the outside and gooey on the inside, we take them off the tip of the stick and smoosh them between graham crackers with half of a Hershey's chocolate bar to make s'mores.

I eat three of them and only lose two marshmallows in the fire. Tobin loses three but eats five.

Charlie tells silly ghost stories that are more funny than scary, and it makes me forget that we're deep in the woods just waiting to be eaten by something ferocious or poisoned by something venomous.

Tobin is the first to fall asleep, still curled up in his lawn chair next to the fire.

"Tired?" Charlie asks me. He's using his pocketknife to whittle a lump of wood he found on the ground.

"No," I say. "Not really."

I stare into the crackling fire.

The logs are turning white and black as the bright orange flames dance over the embers, moving to the pop-and-crackle beat. Even though the air is cold now, the fire fills the small space around us. When a patch of cool air slips through and wraps around my shoulders, I shiver. Charlie looks up then, takes off his blue Windbreaker, and hands it to me.

"Thanks," I say.

I pull it on. It smells like him. Like Irish Spring and the bottle of Old Spice he keeps on the bathroom counter. The lump of wood in his hand looks like it could either end up being a bear or maybe . . . Mount Rushmore.

Still too soon to tell.

It's quiet except for the crackling and popping of the flittering flames. It seems like it takes forever for anyone to say anything while I watch the logs and Charlie carves.

"I don't know what your mother's told you about us," he starts, not looking at me.

"Nothing," I say.

Then it's quiet again for a real long time. His eyebrows are low as he concentrates on his carving.

"We didn't get along after her mother died," he tells me, and then clears his throat.

I look up at him.

"Why not?" I ask.

"Well . . . ," he starts. "I suppose it was because we were both just . . . sad . . . you know. We didn't know what to do with all our sadness about losing someone who meant so much, someone we shouldn't have had to lose. Someone we weren't expecting to lose. Everything changed. I know you know what I mean by that."

I do, and I tell him so.

"Yes," I say.

"So we let all our sad and mad feelings take over, and instead of loving and supporting each other, we hurt each other with our words."

I think about the volcano inside me and all the spewing lava that comes out when I don't even mean it to. It makes me wonder if Mama had a volcano inside her too.

*Elizabeth Lilly Witt.*

I swallow hard.

"I can't imagine how difficult it must be to lose her the way you did," Charlie says, clearing his throat a bunch of times. "To be all alone, watch her get so sick and not be able to do anything to help her. A day doesn't go by that I don't wish I could have done something to help her. If I had known, maybe I could have . . . well, anyway, I should have been there to take care of her . . . and you."

"I took care of her just fine." I point to myself. "I did it. I didn't need anyone to do it."

I swallow again, but the lump just keeps getting bigger, and now my eyes are watering up too.

I wipe at them with my forearm.

"I'm sure you did a great job of taking care of her, Lem." Charlie's voice sounds shaky on the last word, and he clears his throat again. "I just wish I could have been there too. I miss your mom more than I can tell you. Losing her now is like losing her twice for me. I had always hoped we could repair our relationship and become a family again . . . but now I know that will never happen."

I sniff and wipe at my eyes again. A log crumbles and breaks in two, making a loud popping sound that sends sparks leaping toward the sky. I watch the fire, trying to swallow away the lump that just won't go down.

"Her name was Rebecca."

"Yes," he says after another long pause. "Rebecca Genevieve Witt." He says it slowly, in a way that makes it sound like a real important name that he wants the universe to remember.

*Rebecca Genevieve Witt.*

"Is that your wedding ring?" I point to the bright silver ring on his hand.

"Yep," he says. "And I keep hers on a chain around my neck too." He pulls out a thin chain from under his collar and shows me.

It's a smaller bright silver ring with a diamond on it.

"Makes me feel closer to her."

I wish I had a ring of Mama's to carry around my neck too.

"How . . . ," I start, but my voice comes out all squeaky and high.

I clear my throat now too.

"How do you learn to breathe again?" I ask.

I wonder if he knows what I mean. About the sadness inside me. Sometimes I feel so sad inside, I don't think I'll ever feel good again.

*Not ever.*

And it scares me. Like I'm drowning in sadness quicksand, and if I don't get out, no one will ever find me. And what's worse . . .

It feels like no one is even looking.

Charlie stops his carving when I ask my question and looks straight at me. I can see that his eyes are as watery as mine are.

"One day at a time, Lem. Sometimes . . ." He blinks back the tears. "Sometimes, it's one moment at a time."

I stare at the flames, and Charlie goes back to his Mount Rushmore. Maybe it's a Bigfoot he's carving out of that thing.

"Good to talk about it," he says.

I wipe my eyes again with my arm and sniff.

I point to the carving. "What is that thing, anyway?"

He looks at it and holds it out, examining it in the light of the fire.

"I whittle until the wood tells *me* what it is."

"What is the wood saying?" I ask.

He examines it. Then he pretends to listen to it.

"She's pretty quiet tonight." He smiles. "What does it look like to *you*?"

I squint and turn my head to the side, then close the other eye and wrinkle my nose.

"A bunny," I decide.

He raises his eyebrows, looks at it again.

"I do believe you may just be right."

"Mama loves bunnies," I say, thinking of the gray ceramic bunnies she had on the rooftop deck at home. Bunnies dancing. Bunnies hopping. There was even one bunny holding a big red heart.

"Yes," he says softly. "She sure did."

# 17

# DR. CHARLIE

"It's gangrene."

Tobin and Charlie are leaning over me the next morning, examining the scrape on my knee that I got when I fell on my way back from the pee spot. I'm not going to candy-coat it, either: it's a gusher.

Bloody in the middle and all green on the edges. That's how I know it's gangrene.

"They'll probably have to amputate," I say.

Charlie and Tobin look at each other, and Tobin slaps his forehead and shakes his head.

"It's not gangrene," he says.

"Are you blind?" I point to it. "It's green, see?"

"It's a grass stain, you dope."

"That's what *you* know," I say. "My fingernails are completely numb, and they say that's the first sign."

"Who feels their fingernails?" Tobin demands. "And who are *they*, anyway?"

"They," I say. "Them. The people."

"What people?"

"Is this really what you want to be talking about right now when I'm at death's door? I need an ambulance and a doctor before I lose more than just my leg."

Tobin blows air out of his mouth and looks at Charlie.

"She's ruining the whole trip," he says, and then he turns to me. "You're ruining the *whole* trip, I hope you know."

"Okay, now," Charlie says calmly. "First off, Lem, I think you're going to survive, and so will your leg. We just need to clean it up, is all."

"I really think a doctor should do it," I tell him.

"He *is* a doctor," Tobin says.

I watch Charlie pull a first aid kit out of a brown paper grocery bag. He opens the box and takes out some cotton balls and a Band-Aid and some clear liquid in a bottle.

"A real doctor?"

"Retired," he says, dabbing a cotton ball with the liquid.

"Oh."

"This might sting a little, but I think it will save you an amputation."

I take a deep breath and squeeze my eyes closed.

"Ready," I tell him.

"Here we go," he says.

As soon as he touches me, I feel the sting.

"Ouch!" I say, jumping. "It burns! It burns!"

Charlie blows on it, which takes some of the sting away. The clear liquid also cleans up the green stain.

I guess they were right. No gangrene. Just grass.

"It'll be okay in a minute," Charlie says, taking a breath and blowing again. "I think you're going to live." He dabs and blows again. "How are those fingernails doing?"

I check them.

"Still can't feel them."

He smiles.

"Perfect."

I guess he's right about everything.

This time.

But that doesn't mean there isn't a bug still burrowing into my insides, or that I don't have malaria from the zillion mosquito bites on my arms and legs. I slap my neck and flick another mosquito off my finger.

A zillion and one.

Not to mention, I found out I'm allergic to expeditions. I didn't know I was allergic to expeditions, since I've never been on one before. But clearly I'm allergic, because I've sneezed thirty-two times alone since the sun finally showed its face above the trees. My record is eight sneezes in a row without a single break.

Sneeze.

Thirty-three.

I wonder how many sneezes in a row a body can take before you actually achoo yourself to death. Maybe I'll be the first. It was what woke me up this morning, and everyone else, too, since we all had our sleeping bags lined up in the same tent. Charlie said I was a good alarm clock and then put some dabs of white cream on each mosquito bite.

Tobin didn't agree.

I figure this out because of all the eye-rolling and the forehead-slapping, and also because he tells me so once we get going on our after-breakfast hike.

"How are we supposed to come up on any Bigfoot with you making all that racket?" Tobin yells back at me over his shoulder. "You're scaring them all off."

Charlie is leading us through the woods with a large backpack hanging from his shoulders. Tobin is in front of me with the Polaroid camera around his neck, and I'm following with Tobin's movie camera hanging from mine.

"Like I'm doing it on purpose?" I sneeze again. "I can't help that I'm allergic to expeditions."

"Well, you're ruining everything," Tobin says.

"That's so rude," I say. "You don't think I'd have rather stayed with Mrs. Dickerson, sipping tea and munching on cookies, instead of stomping around in the woods looking for a giant ape?"

Sneeze.

"Again with the complaining."

"*You're* the one complaining." I smack another mosquito on my forehead. "If *I* was going to complain, I'd complain about losing my blood to all the insects of the forest." I smack my leg. "But you don't hear me saying that, do you? No, you don't."

"If you'd let Charlie spray you with the Off!, they'd leave you alone."

"That stink-in-a-can? I'd gag if I had to smell like that all day."

Another eye roll.

"Okay, now," Charlie says. "It's daylight, anyhow. We know they're nocturnal animals, and coming upon an actual Bigfoot isn't likely anyway. So let's keep an eye out for evidence. A footprint, hair, scat, something like that."

"Patterson and Gimlin filmed their Bigfoot in the middle of the day," Tobin reminds him. "In Bluff Creek, *anything* is possible."

Then he glares at me again.

"Anything *would* have been possible," he mutters under his breath.

The volcano inside me bubbles up a low heat, making me want to snatch that stupid hat off his head and smack him with it.

But I don't.

"What's scat?" I holler up to Charlie instead.

"Number two," Tobin says.

"What?"

"It's number two. You know, poop."

Did he just say what I think he said?

"So, not only are we looking for a big ape in the woods," I say, "we're also looking for its number two? That's the most disgusting thing I've ever heard."

"Everything poops," Tobin says. "What's the big deal about it?"

"The big deal is you don't usually hunt for it in the woods."

Charlie stops then and pulls his backpack off his shoulders.

"What are we doing?" I ask.

Charlie unzips the pack and pulls out a hand-drawn map

and an old magazine article from 1967 about Roger Patterson. Charlie and Tobin drew the rough map based on information in the article to try to find exactly where the Bigfoot was filmed. They've been studying it all week.

"I think we're here." Charlie points to a spot on the paper. "We need to head this way for another mile or so. Then we should be right up at the sandbar where they filmed her."

"Yep," Tobin says. "I think so too."

"How's everyone doing? Everybody okay?" Charlie looks at me.

Both Tobin and I nod.

"Let's keep going, then," Charlie says, lugging his heavy pack back over his shoulders. "I've got a good feeling we might just find something today."

• • •

A zillion miles later, we finally stop. My feet are tired, and my nose is still running, and my mosquito bites are even itchier. But I won't complain.

Not out loud, anyway.

"I think this is it!" Tobin shouts, pointing straight ahead. "Charlie? That looks like the dry creek bed. What do you think? Right up there! Through that clearing there!"

They study the map closely, and then look at the trees, then the map, and then the trees again. I yawn and lean against the big trunk of an old oak.

"I think so." Charlie strokes his beard.

Tobin starts to run.

"That's the sandbar there." He's pointing. "Right? This looks right, right?"

I yawn again.

"Did we bring any snacks?" I ask Charlie.

"For criminy sake, Lemonade." Tobin turns around to face me with his hands on his hips. "We're only making cryptozoological history here. Our names might just be in every history book ever produced from here on out, and you're talking Twinkies?"

"What can I say? Making history makes me hungry."

Charlie digs a Twinkie out of his backpack and hands it to me. It's squished, with filling all squeezed out of the three holes in the bottom and smeared against the wrapper.

"It's all smooshed," I say.

"Tastes the same." He smiles.

I take it and sit down in the grass under the oak while Charlie and Tobin examine the area to see if it's official or not. I carefully peel the plastic wrap off the golden cake to save for licking later, and then devour the Twinkie in three bites. Who knew expeditions could make a person so hungry?

"This is where Roger Patterson stumbles with the camera, here!" Tobin points.

"And where she turns around and looks right into the camera, here!" Charlie says.

I watch them while I start on the plastic wrap, licking every last bit of the sweet filling. They study the map, then check for signs it's a match. This tree and that rock and this clearing and so on.

When I'm done licking the plastic wrap clean, I scrunch it in a ball and put it in the pocket of Charlie's Windbreaker, still wrapped around me from last night. I rest my head on my knees, my eyes feeling heavier with each blink. My lids beg me to let them stay shut each time my eyelashes touch.

"You walk the path the Bigfoot did, and I'll take pictures," Tobin suggests to Charlie. "That's good . . . yeah, now turn and look back at me . . . riiiight there . . ." Tobin clicks the camera.

I sneeze, waking my eyes up for good.

"Why don't you just scare away all the critters of the forest?" Tobin hollers at me.

My volcano wants to tell him to shut up.

But I don't.

I stand up and brush the dirt off my backside instead. And that's when I notice it.

Is it?

It can't be. I squint real hard and take another look.

I think it *is*.

# 18

# A MIDTARSAL BREAK

"Hey!" I call over to Tobin and Charlie, waving my arms frantically. "Hey! I think I found something over here!"

They're so busy with their stupid map and re-creating the Patterson-Gimlin film that they don't even hear me. I crouch down to get a closer look at the dried mud next to where I've been sitting. Then I get down on my hands and knees and eyeball the ground just like Tobin does.

I carefully touch what looks like indentations with the tips of my fingers. The mud is hardened, but the marks are as clear as day.

A footprint.

There's a big toe and a smaller one and another smaller one and another. All five toes. Even a heel. An entire footprint. I'm sure of it. And it's humongous, too, more than a whole ruler for sure. At least a ruler and a half.

Then I see another footprint.

And another one!

"Hey!" I say, louder this time. "I really think I found something here!"

They both stop talking and turn to look at me from over at the sandbar.

"Footprints!" I shout at them.

I lean down and touch the prints again. The afternoon sun is shining high up above me, sprinkling the forest with light through leaves and pine needles. In that light, shining down from the sky, I have found my very first evidence of the elusive Bigfoot.

Me.

Lemonade Liberty Witt.

Assistant Bigfoot Detective.

• • •

"I don't see anything," Tobin says, aiming his flashlight on the ground in the shade of the brush and trees and grasses while Charlie hovers over his left shoulder.

I'm on my hands and knees pointing out my discovery, and all of a sudden, I don't even care about my mosquito bites or the scrape on my knee or that I'm dirty, tired, and hungry, or that I have to go to the bathroom again and the toilet paper is a zillion miles in the opposite direction.

"See here?" I say with my face close to the ground, studying the mud in the extra light of Tobin's flashlight. "It looks like it could be a footprint in the mud. Aren't these toes here? And maybe a heel there? Look at this one, and this one over here." I point. "See them? I think I even see dental ridges on this big toe. Right here. Can you see it? Get your magnifying glass."

"It's dermal ridges, not dental ridges," Tobin reminds me, getting on his knees too and shining the flashlight closer.

"Oh, man," he breathes. "It *is*. I see them."

He pulls his magnifying glass out of his back pocket and eyes them, nose to the dirt. Charlie looks around for additional signs by carefully lifting branches and peering under bushes.

"More prints under the bushes to the left," he calls from behind a tree. "Two sets. A set of large footprints, and a set of little ones."

"Same thing over here!" Tobin exclaims. "Adult and a juvenile, you think, Charlie?"

"Juvenile?" I say.

"See?" Tobin pushes the bush up to show me. "Small feet next to the big ones. Don't you think, Charlie?"

"Could be," Charlie says, placing his backpack on the ground and unzipping it.

"The Bigfoot that Roger Patterson filmed out here was a female," Tobin explains. "Some think a mother. Maybe it's her. Maybe it's the same one. Wouldn't that be *spectacular*? Wouldn't it, Charlie?" Tobin beams.

"A mother?" I ask. "How do you know that?"

"Why do you have to ask so many questions?" Tobin blurts out, continuing to eyeball the prints with his magnifying glass. "Why can't you just accept what I tell you?"

"I accept it," I say. "I just want to know why. Is there some kind of law about asking questions?"

He ignores me.

"Tobin."

"Fine. It's because she has . . . you know . . . ex-extra parts," he stammers without looking at me.

"*Extra parts?* What kind of extra parts?"

"You know . . . the girly kind . . . the, ah . . . the ones up top there." He waves a hand over his front while a slow storm of red creeps over his cheeks. "Now quit asking so many questions and stop stomping around all over the mud—you're going to ruin the prints."

"*I'm* the one who found them, remember?" I remind him. "Me. I'm not ruining anything."

He ignores me again.

"What do you think, Charlie? Should we cast them?" Tobin asks.

Charlie nods, pulling packets of white powder and a canteen of water out of his backpack.

"What are you going to do with all that?" I ask.

"He's mixing up some plaster of Paris; then we'll pour it in the prints, it will harden, and we'll be able to take the shape of the print back with us to study it further. The rain will eventually wash these away, and we won't have anything left. But we should document the find with pictures, too."

Tobin holds his camera close to the ground and starts taking picture after picture.

"What should I do?" I ask.

"Document with that." He points to the movie camera still around my neck. "Channel Four News might want to use the discovery footage for a breaking news alert."

I nod and find the power button on the side of the camera. It makes a soft humming noise. I point it in the direction of Tobin and Charlie working to preserve the prints in the mud.

"Tobin Sky, founder and president of Bigfoot Detectives Inc., and his trusty assistant, Lemonade Liberty Witt, have just discovered what are believed to be possible Bigfoot prints in the forests of Bluff Creek," I announce in a reporter's voice. "Lemonade Liberty Witt was on her first expedition when she came upon the prints. If it wasn't for her quick observational skills, the prints might have been left undiscovered for eternity, or washed away by rain. . . ."

Tobin peers at me over his wire-rims with an annoyed look on his face.

"It's a *silent* picture," he tells me.

"I know it," I say.

"So just film it. We don't need the commentary."

I can't help but smile.

"Tobin Sky will surely make Lemonade Liberty Witt partner after this amazing find on her part," I continue. "It's highly likely that *60 Minutes* will want the first interview with Miss Witt. Maybe she will even take over as lead detective at the agency before the summer has ended—"

"Charlie!" Tobin hollers.

I have to cover my mouth so he doesn't see me snickering.

● ● ●

So, it turns out there's something even better than prints with dermal ridges.

Footprints with a midtarsal break.

We watch Charlie mix the murky mess of white powder and water together and then pour it into the dried, muddy footprints. There isn't enough for all the prints, so Charlie just does two of the very best big ones, where you can see the clearest outline of the foot, and one of the very best little ones. When the first one is dry enough to pick up from the mud, Charlie reaches down and pulls it out of the earth to show us.

"There it is!" Tobin exclaims. "The midtarsal break! I knew it! I knew it!" He jumps up and down. "Are you getting this on film?"

"What the heck is a midtarsal break?" I ask, focusing the camera in the direction of the cast footprint.

Charlie points to the middle of the cast. "It's a flexible joint in the foot where humans have a stiff arch. It allows primates to have better balance and flexibility over rough terrain, like jungles and forests and such," he says, brushing loose grass, sticks, and pebbles off the newly hardened foot statues.

I think Tobin is going to have a stroke, he's so happy about what we found. Correction: what I found.

Me.

Lemonade Liberty Witt.

Assistant Bigfoot Detective.

"Patterson, Gimlin, and Sky!" he exclaims. "I'm going to be the most famous discoverer since the Patterson-Gimlin film."

"Patterson, Gimlin, Sky, and Witt," I correct him. "Don't forget who actually found these things. You walked right by them. If I hadn't stopped to suck the filling off a Twinkie wrapper, they would have gone unnoticed forever."

Tobin thinks about it.

"All right," he says. "Patterson, Gimlin, Sky, and Witt."

Charlie sighs and smiles down at us.

"It was a good day, Bigfoot hunters," he says. "We make a good team."

Tobin and I look at each other, and we smile too.

# 19

# ASSISTANT DETECTIVE
# EXTRAORDINAIRE

With Expedition: Bluff Creek a stunning success, thanks to my amazing investigative skills, Tobin and I help Charlie set up a big display in the glass case near the register at Bigfoot Souvenirs and More that Monday morning. While Charlie works on setting up the footprints, we're lying on our stomachs near the fireplace, coloring a giant map of Bluff Creek for the backdrop.

The bell on the door rings. I don't really even pay attention until I hear this weird noise come out of Tobin's throat.

"Good morning, boys!" Charlie calls from behind the counter. "Did you come to hear about our fantastic discovery out at Bluff Creek?"

Tobin ducks his head lower and keeps coloring without saying anything. He's got the greens: grass and forest. I've got the yellows and blues: sun and sky.

"Yeah," says one boy. "We heard about the footprints. Well, everyone has. It's all anyone is talking about, really."

There are two of them. Probably the same age as us. One with a buzz cut and a Styx T-shirt, and the other with long bangs that he keeps swinging out of his eyes.

The phone rings in the back room.

"I'll be just a minute," Charlie tells them. "Maybe Tobin and Lem can start."

Charlie steps around the counter and into the back room.

"Bigfoot Souvenirs and More. How can I help you today?" we hear him say into the receiver.

The boys shuffle in our direction, stopping next to where we're coloring. They look down at us with stupid smirks on their faces. The one with the buzz cut puts a Nike toe on my sun.

"You're on my sun," I inform him.

He doesn't budge, still smirking down at me.

"So, what's your story?" He juts a chin in my direction.

Tobin makes that noise in the back of his throat again.

"Don't you have any manners?" I ask the boy with the buzz cut, picking up his toe and moving it myself.

"What?" he asks.

"*Manners*," I say again, slower this time. "You're generally supposed to acknowledge someone with some kind of greeting before bombarding them with rude questions."

The boys look at each other and laugh.

I know that laugh. I've heard it before.

Tobin makes another weird sound and then starts scribbling harder. I just know he's going to shred the paper straight through and ruin the whole thing.

"Oh, excuse me, please, Miss Fancy Pants. How are you doing this fine morning, and by the way . . . what's your story?" Buzz Cut asks while he curtsies, holding out a pretend skirt.

Bangs laughs at him and swings his head right.

"Better, but still needs work," I tell him, leaning back and examining my swirling clouds.

"She's Tobin's new *girlfriend*," Bangs says.

"Wrong!" Tobin snaps his head up.

I sigh, set my crayon down, and look up at the two boys.

"I just moved here from San Francisco," I say. "Not that it's any of your business."

They laugh again.

"Huh," Buzz Cut says. "Seems to me like you're spending a lot of time with Tobin here. In my book, that makes you his *girlfriend*."

"She is not!" Tobin shouts again.

"In your book?" I ask. "So that's just the one, then? One book you've read? *Singular?*" I smile.

He glares at me, and I know that he knows that I know it was them on the other end of the green phone that day.

"Do you kiss her on the lips while you sit on Charlie's porch swing, Tobin?" Bangs asks, making kissing noises.

Tobin pops up from the floor and glares at them with his fists clenched at his sides.

Thumbs sticking straight up.

"Yeah, well, you . . . you're just . . . you and . . . why don't you just go and shut up!" Tobin finally spits out.

Brutal.

I wonder if he knows that as far as comebacks go, he's the worst. He needs a serious lesson. Lucky for him, he's got me.

"Listen here," I start. "Why don't you and Moron Number Two here go and—"

"Kids." Charlie comes out of the back room. "Is there a problem?"

"No, sir." Buzz Cut shoots an award-winning smile in Charlie's direction.

"Just ignore them, Tobin," I whisper, grabbing the Midnight Blue from the box. "Who cares what they think, anyway?"

Charlie is by Tobin's side now.

"Problem?" he asks again, putting a hand on Tobin's shoulder.

"Oh, not at all, sir." Buzz Cut's lips stretch wide over his teeth. "We just came in to see what all the talk around town is about. We heard you cast those prints. That right?"

"You boys come on over this way, and I'll show you what we found." Charlie smiles. As he guides the two doofuses to the glass case, he looks over his shoulder at Tobin and winks.

Tobin gets back down on the floor and starts coloring again, scribbling green furiously on the paper.

"Hey." I grab his arm. "Stop. What are you doing? You're going to rip it."

"They make me so mad," he hisses at me. Then he stops coloring and takes his glasses off and wipes at his eyes.

"Those two idiots?" I ask, pointing up at the counter. "Don't give them the time of day. They just want to get a rise out of you. If you show them you don't care, they'll leave you alone."

"You don't understand," he tells me.

"Well, one thing I can say for sure is that you're the absolute worst at comebacks in the history of the world. I mean really bad," I say, holding my nose. "Like stink-o-rino."

He smiles then and even laughs a little.

"I just get so flustered that I can't get the words in my head to come out of my mouth."

"Well, good thing you have me to coach you. I'll give you some real good zingers too. I'm the comeback queen in the city."

"You'd do that?"

"Sure." I shrug. "You know they're really just jealous, right?"

"No." He shakes his head. "That's not it."

"Oh, yeah."

"Of what?"

"Not everyone makes founder and president of their own company by the fifth grade," I say.

Tobin thinks hard about that.

Then I see the corners of his mouth curl up in a smile.

# 20

# PROFESSOR JERROD MALCOLM, PHD

It's already July.

It's been thirty-one days.

Thirty-one whole days since I first walked up Charlie's porch steps.

My room looks a lot different than it did that first day. A lot less old-man study and a lot more almost-eleven-year-old-girl bedroom. Every week, Charlie brings home something new for my room that he orders from the Sears catalog. Last week, he surprised me with a fluffy rainbow comforter.

Just like the one I have at home.

That social worker who drove me here hasn't come back yet, but she's called three times. Once to talk to me and twice to talk to Charlie. I don't know what she talked to Charlie about because he used the phone in his bedroom to talk to her. But with me she just talked about the weather and asked lots of questions about Willow Creek. She told me she'd be up to see me later this month and asked if I wanted her to bring me anything from San Francisco. I told her an order of Mr. Chin's crispy fried egg rolls. She just laughed.

I guess she thought I was kidding.

On Monday morning, after Charlie leaves for work, Tobin and I head to the Bigfoot Headquarters. We've been getting busier and busier since word spread about our find in Bluff Creek. And Tobin is even getting used to me changing things.

Kind of.

He unlocks the side door of the garage, and we can see before he even pulls the string on the single lightbulb that there are messages blinking on the answering machine.

Blink. Blink. Blink.

"There are three messages." Tobin looks at me.

"Play them," I say, leaning an elbow on the desk to listen.

He pushes the Play button.

Beeeeeeeep.

"Hello, my favorite Bigfoot hunters. This is Mrs. Dickerson. I have a sighting to report again this morning. This time, I'm sure I saw one crossing the road in front of my car at dusk last night right here on Brannan Mountain Road. I think you should come out as soon as you get this message to see if you can cast for footprints. And I just took a pan of fudge cookies out of the oven for you."

Beeeeeeeep.

"Tobin and Lemonade sitting in a tree. K-I-S-S-I-N-G. First comes love. Then comes marriage. Then comes Baby in—"

Tobin pushes Stop, and his cheeks are redder than the

Venetian Red in the Crayola box that we used for the campfire on our Bluff Creek map.

"Just ignore them," I remind him. "There's one more message." I point to the blinking light.

He fast-forwards.

Beeeeeeeep.

"Hello? Hello? Is there someone there? Oh, ah, my name is Professor Jerrod Malcolm. I teach anatomy and anthropology at Idaho State University. I understand you have some plaster casts from Bluff Creek? I've been told they may include a midtarsal break? I'm wondering if I can come down and examine them. Please call me back at—"

Tobin looks up again, this time with wide eyes, and I bet if I could see myself in a mirror right this second, mine would be saucers too.

* * *

Professor Malcolm meets us at Bigfoot Souvenirs and More on that very next Saturday. I wear a sundress and the white sandals with the gold buckles on the heels that Mama got me from Hanson's Shoes in the city. I attach my handmade badge with the clumped-up Elmer's to the front of my dress and look in the mirror above the bathroom sink to make sure it's straight.

### LEMONADE LIBERTY WITT
#### Assistant Bigfoot Detective

Tobin shows up at breakfast wearing the same stupid thing he always does. Khaki shorts and a red T-shirt and his safari hat. He looks at me funny when he sees my dress.

"What's with the dress?"

"I want to make a good impression. Couldn't you have dressed up some?" I ask.

"We're not going to church."

"Still, it's kind of a big deal, don't you think?"

"He's coming to look at Bigfoot prints. What does he care about what I'm wearing?" Tobin says.

Later that morning at Bigfoot Souvenirs and More, the bell on the door dings and a tall man with a briefcase pushes it open and peeks inside.

"Good morning!" Charlie calls out.

"Good morning to you all!" Professor Malcolm smiles, closing the door behind him.

He has short blond hair and a short blond beard to match, and he's wearing a red T-shirt and khaki shorts. I glance over at Tobin, and he's giving me the biggest I-told-you-so look you can imagine.

"Welcome! Welcome!" Charlie calls out. "Please, join us over here."

Charlie has all the Bigfoot plaster casts lined up on the hearth of the stone fireplace in the center of the room. We all grab an overstuffed pillow on the floor and sit in a circle.

"Here they are." Charlie motions toward the footprints.

"I see," Professor Malcolm says, pulling a magnifying glass from his back pocket. "They're amazing."

Tobin watches Professor Malcolm with the biggest, goofiest smile on his face that I've ever seen.

"See the midtarsal break here?" Tobin points.

"Yes, I see it, Tobin." Professor Malcolm eyeballs it closer. "It's magnificent. Just magnificent."

This time I'm beaming too.

"I found them," I tell him, pointing to myself. "Me, I'm the one."

"Well, she may have seen them first, but Charlie and I cast them. I'm actually the founder and president of Bigfoot Detectives Inc. here in Willow Creek. This is Lemonade, my assistant," Tobin clarifies, pulling his crumpled business card from his front pocket. "My card."

"Yeah, but I found them," I tell Tobin.

"Yeah, but you wouldn't have found them if I hadn't hired you on as an employee," Tobin says.

"Still, it was me—" I start.

Professor Malcolm smiles at Charlie.

"Well, I think you've both come upon an amazing discovery here. Something that may offer more proof to the rest of the world that Bigfoot actually exists. It seems to me that you two make a great team."

Tobin and I look at each other.

"Yes, sir," I tell him. "We do."

"May I take one of these with me for further examination? I can return it to you after my testing is complete."

"Of course," Charlie tells him. "Please do. We are just so excited to have you here to be a part of our find."

"Thank you very much," Professor Malcolm says, inspecting the store. "You have quite a place here."

"Thank you again." Charlie smiles.

"I see your sign there. Take a story and leave a story. Who wants to start and let me know how exactly you all came to acquire these amazing prints?"

"I can," I tell him, standing up and straightening the front of my dress. I clear my throat and take a deep breath.

"It all started with a Twinkie—" I say.

Tobin hits his forehead with his hand and shakes his head at me.

# 21

# TOBIN'S DAD

I yawn a long yawn.

"I say we call it a day," I tell Tobin with my chin in my hand.

He looks at me over his glasses. He's sitting on the riding lawn mower, shuffling through his yellow legal pad. I'm at the desk, waiting for the phone to ring and rereading the four letters I've gotten from San Francisco so far.

One from Erika Vass, one from Lisa S., and two from Miss Cotton. Miss Cotton even sent me some pictures that she took of us together when I was staying with her. I stuck them to the wall above my bed with Scotch tape.

There's one of us planting vegetables on her rooftop garden, one of us eating Mr. Chin's fried egg rolls, and one of just her smiling into the camera. She reminds me of Mama, except she's younger and her hair is straight, not curly, and brown, not red. But she's pretty like Mama even without lipstick or eye shadow or plucking her eyebrows into skinny lines like some women do. Mama and Miss Cotton wore Birkenstocks instead of high heels and flowy cotton skirts instead of tight ones, and they wore their long hair down their backs instead of wrapping it up in a fancy knot at the back of their necks. But the biggest reason she reminds me of Mama is her smile. It's the brightest smile you've ever seen. She grins with her whole face, so big that her lips almost disappear because all her front teeth are showing. It was that smile that made me love her the minute I walked into her fourth-grade classroom. And it's that smile that makes her most like Mama.

Today is a slow and boring rainy Thursday at the Bigfoot Detectives Headquarters, without one single sighting to investigate.

"Not one call today," I say. "Not even Mrs. Dickerson with a pan of cookies." I yawn again. "Must be the rain. Let's watch television or something."

"Okay," Tobin says. "We have leftover chocolate cake in the fridge. Want to go to my house?"

It's the very first time Tobin has ever invited me over to his house. Since his mom is always working, we usually just stay at Charlie's house or hang out at the store.

"Sure." I shrug. "You have ice cream, too?"

"Yeah," he says. "No vanilla, though, only strawberry. My mom only ever buys strawberry, even though vanilla goes best with chocolate cake. I tell her that, but she never buys it."

"Okay by me, I eat all kinds," I reassure him.

After locking up the Bigfoot Headquarters, we head across the street to Tobin's house. It's a lot like Charlie's. It has a front porch wrapped all around too, except their house is green with white trim, instead of white with yellow trim.

Inside, it smells sweet, like chocolate and cinnamon, and also like flowery Lysol and a little bit of bleach. It's very clean and orderly, with no dishes in the sink, and even the mail is tucked neatly in a basket, instead of in a messy pile on the counter like it is at Charlie's.

"Want to see my room?" Tobin asks.

I shrug.

"Sure," I say.

He leads me up the long flight of steps, which is just past the kitchen. When we reach the top step, I see a long hall with three doors. The first door is the bathroom. There is purple flowered wallpaper covering the walls and one big fluffy yellow rug on the floor.

"That's my mom's room," Tobin says, pointing to the next door down the hall.

The door is partly open, so I peek inside.

The bed isn't made, but it's only messy on one side. There's a silver picture frame on the nightstand. In it is Tobin's mom in a beautiful, flowing wedding dress holding a bouquet of flowers. Next to her is the same man with reddish-brown curls who was in the picture I found in Tobin's leather case. Except this time, the man isn't leaned up against a car; he's in a suit, and his curls are parted down the middle and slicked down with a bunch of goop.

I push the door open a little bit farther and slip inside.

"Hey," Tobin protests. "What are you doing?"

"Who's this?" I ask him, picking up the frame from the nightstand.

He doesn't say anything for a few seconds.

"My dad," he finally says. "Now put it back."

"Where is he?"

"I don't know."

"What do you mean you don't know? Did he leave?"

"For Vietnam," Tobin says.

"He's a soldier?"

"Yeah, he was drafted for the war five years ago and just never came home." Tobin takes the frame from my hand and places it carefully back on the nightstand.

"Did he die?"

"We don't know." He stares at the picture.

"When's the last time you saw him?"

"He left the summer before I started kindergarten. I only remember some things about him, like when he used to push me on the swings at the park sometimes. And the time we had an Easter egg hunt and we collected all the eggs together. Mom hid them in the yard and around the house. There was even one in the dryer. Dad found that one. And before he left, he gave me a silver dollar."

"Did you love him?"

"What kind of question is that?" Tobin demands.

"I don't know, I—"

"Of course I love him. Do you love your mom?"

Even though they sound like words, they feel more like little stab wounds in my gut.

"Sorry," he says. "I . . . um, I didn't mean to . . ."

I guess Tobin has his own volcano.

"I know it," I say.

"How did she die?" he asks me then. "I mean, I know she had cancer and all, but . . ."

"In the hospital," I say. "They couldn't treat it anymore and she got real skinny and real sick and lost all her hair. It was a Monday when she stopped getting out of bed and her best friend, Catt, who came over to help make meals for us, said she needed to go back in. Her real name is Catherine, but no one ever calls her that."

"Did you see her? I mean after . . ."

I nod and then feel that lump coming up in my throat. That same one that always does.

"Is your room the next door?" I ask him.

"Sorry," he says. "I mean, I don't know—"

"It's all right," I say, brushing past him.

He doesn't say anything, he just follows.

I push open the third door. It's perfect. Everything in its place. Not that I would expect anything different.

His bed is made tight. So tight you could probably use it as a trampoline. It has a gray bedspread, and there are matching curtains hanging at the window. On his dresser, green army men are lined up in a perfect row ready for their call to action. There's a poster on the wall of Apollo 11 blasting into space in 1969 on its first trip to the moon, and a mini red rocket night-light next to the bed. There are dark wooden cube letters over the bed that spell out T-O-B-I-N.

"You like space stuff?"

"Yeah," he says, sitting on the edge of the bed.

There's a stack of books on the nightstand. Surprisingly enough, books about something other than Bigfoot. I go down the list of titles.

*The Adventures of Huckleberry Finn* . . . *Sing Down the Moon* . . . and something about electromagnetic fields.

I pull open the closet door, and it creaks in protest. Inside are red T-shirts as far as the eye can see, all lined up perfectly on hangers.

On Tobin's nightstand is a picture of him and his dad holding a basket filled with colorful eggs. I pick up the picture.

The man is smiling with lots of teeth showing and he's holding Tobin's hand. "He looks nice," I say.

"He is. At least what I can remember."

"What's his name?"

"Scotty," he says. "Scotty Tobin Sky."

*Scotty Tobin Sky.*

I look up at Tobin and he looks back at me. "It sounds like an important name," I tell him.

He nods.

"Wish I could've met him."

"You will," he says. "When he gets back."

I stare at him.

"What do you mean? You think he's still coming home?"

"Yeah." He pushes up his glasses.

"You really think he might?"

"I don't think it, I know it. Every day I wonder if this is the day he'll walk through the front door."

• • •

That night I can't sleep. I can't stop thinking about Tobin and his dad.

*Scotty Tobin Sky.*

Part of me feels jealous that he gets to hope that his dad is still alive and will still come home. The other part of me feels sorry for him that he doesn't know for sure.

I wish I didn't know for sure.

I wish I knew Mama might come back to me.

I wish . . . I wish . . . more than anything, I wish she would.

A low roll of thunder answers me.

"Mama?" I whisper. "If God really knew how much I miss you, he would send you back to me. I still need you, Mama."

*Elizabeth Lilly Witt.*

There's a windy rain that clicks against the window, and every three seconds there's a flash and then another roll of thunder. The storm is getting closer. I lie on my side under the fluffy rainbow comforter, staring at the redheaded girl in the frame on the new night table next to my bed.

Charlie never asked me about the empty space on the wall where I swiped the picture.

Another low grumble.

"Mama?"

Click. Click. Click.

The rain answers me, spitting against the window.

I sit up and turn the knob on the lamp next to the bed. A small light glows in the darkness. If I had my glow-in-the-dark stars, I'd have no problem falling asleep. Maybe Charlie would order those from the Sears catalog too.

I sit up in bed and sigh.

The latest book Charlie bought me is on top of the old, rickety trunk at the end of the bed. *Ellen Tebbits*, by Beverly Cleary.

I slip out of bed. The bare-naked floor creaks and groans underneath my toes. I grab the book off the trunk and stare at the worn wood and rusted metal, wondering what might be inside it. Maybe it's something really important and interesting. Or maybe just some more boring, colorless grown-up books. I decide to find out.

On my knees, I wrap my hands around the edge of the trunk and pull, but it doesn't want to budge. Like it's hiding something very important, and it's been hiding it for a very long time, and it isn't ready to share it quite yet.

I push and tug at it until it finally lets go just a little. Then I wiggle and yank until the top pulls up away from the trunk. It creaks and groans, telling me to leave it be. But I keep on wiggling until it makes it all the way up.

The air inside it escapes into the room, an old, musty smell mixed with cedar. When the light reaches the inside of the trunk, my breath sucks in so fast it almost chokes me.

"Oh," I whisper.

I stare at the inside of the trunk, unable to move.

The rain clicks against the window. And a flash lights the room.

When the thunder follows with a loud *craaack*, I jump and slam the lid of the trunk down hard. I scramble back under the covers and pull them tight over my head.

In the hall, I hear heavy footsteps creaking over the floorboards. The doorknob slowly turns.

I know it's him.

"Lem?" Charlie whispers.

I hold my breath and pretend I'm sleeping.

"Lem?" he calls.

I don't move.

## 22

# EGG SALAD FINGERS
# AND ONE HEAVY LOAD

There are three major things that Charlie hasn't figured out about me yet:

1. I hate tomatoes on the egg salad sandwiches that he orders from Diesel's Deli. I always have to pick them off with my fingers.
2. Mama promised me a kitten for my eleventh birthday. I was going to name her Happy.
3. And this one's embarrassing. . . . I never learned to ride a bike.

Number three is the exact reason why I'm hoofing it to Mrs. Dickerson's house. The same day that Debbie took off from the hospital to drive her and Tobin to the nursing home where Tobin's grandma lives down in Redding.

It's hot today after the rain, and humid, too, which makes my curls even frizzier than normal. Just as I'm wishing I had braided my hair in one long braid with the orange and green yarn ribbon, I hear someone calling out behind me.

"Hey, San Fran!"

I turn to see Buzz Cut on a blue bike, pedaling up behind me. I hold my chin high and just keep on walking like I couldn't care less.

"Hey! San Fran!" he calls again, pulling in front of me and whipping his bike in a circle. This wouldn't be a big deal on any other day. Like on a day it didn't pour rain the night before.

But it did, so it is.

And in a matter of a millisecond, I am covered in a fine mist of mud sprayed up from his back tire.

"Are you stupid or something?" I shout at him. "Look what you did!"

"Where you going?"

I put my hands on my hips. "Didn't you even hear what I said?"

"Yeah, I heard you. Where you going?" he asks again, riding slow circles around me as I walk.

"If it was any of your business, maybe I'd tell you, but it's not, so I won't," I say, trying to brush off the mud, which only makes it smear.

"I forgot your name," he says.

"Good," I say, walking past him. "Keep it that way."

He pulls up next to me again, pedaling slow to keep pace with my steps.

"Fruit Punch?"

I ignore him.

"Soda Pop?"

I ignore that one too.

"Strawberry Quik?"

"I can tell by the stupid smile on your face that you think you're funny, but you're wrong about that, too," I inform him.

"Lemonade!" he calls out then. "Right? I'm right, right?"

"Congratulations."

"I think I would have gone with Strawberry Quik. You know, 'cause of the hair and everything."

I glare at him, and he laughs.

"So, where are you going, and why don't you ride your bike?"

"Like I said before. It's none of your business."

"Why are you hanging out with Tobin Sky?"

I don't say one word.

"There's something wrong with that kid, you know. I mean really, what's with that hat, anyway? The kid never takes it off."

"Well, *we* think there's something wrong with *you*." I stop and put my hands on my hips. "It's you, right? With the phone calls?"

He laughs again.

"I don't see what's so funny."

"Keeps us busy in the summer."

"Try rug hooking," I say.

He laughs harder.

"We're playing Kick the Can at Nick French's after lunch," he says, pedaling circles around me again.

"So?"

"So, you can come if you want to."

"Why would I want to do that?"

"You're going to be in Mrs. Santamaria's class, right? Fifth grade? That's J-Man's mom. You'll meet him if you come today. She makes cupcakes for the class when it's your birthday and gives the least amount of homework."

I shrug.

"Well, you can meet some people before school starts. If you want. There's going to be a bunch of us playing."

I think about it.

"I don't know," I say.

"French lives in the blue house, third one down from the library in town. Eighteen oh eight. About one o'clock. Maybe I'll see you there."

I don't say anything as I watch him pedal off, spraying mud like a sprinkler with his back wheel.

● ● ●

At Mrs. Dickerson's, we eat tiny egg salad sandwiches that she calls finger sandwiches, even though they don't look anything like fingers, and we sip chamomile tea with honey from china cups on her front porch.

"Will you tell me more about when Mama was little?" I ask her.

"Oh, honey, I have a million stories."

"I want to know all of them," I tell her, sipping my tea.

"Well, let's see. Did I tell you about the time your mom was the lead in the Easter production at school?"

"The lead in a play?" I ask. "No."

"It was adorable. What was the play?" She rubs her temples to help her find the right memory. "Oh, I can't recall. But it was an Easter play, and she wore a paper bonnet on her head."

I laugh. "A paper bonnet?"

"Well, she couldn't remember her lines halfway through, but she made up an entirely new story. All the other kids just went with it, and the whole second half was improvised. It started off as a play about an Easter bonnet and ended up being a story about saving the animals of the forest. She was always about the animals."

"Still is," I tell her. "You know Mama is a vet in the city?"

"Yes, honey, I do."

"How do you know?"

"Oh, well, Charlie kept close tabs on her even after she left for good. Charlie would take trips to the city and check up on her to make sure she was okay. Then, of course, when you came along, the trips were more frequent."

"He did that? I don't remember ever meeting him."

"You didn't. . . ." She looks off into the woods across the street. "Elizabeth just couldn't get over the past, and he was devastated by that. He wanted so desperately to make amends."

"Well, maybe he didn't try hard enough."

"Oh, he did, honey. Believe me."

"Mama would have forgiven him if he'd tried. If he'd really tried, she would have. Mama was like that."

"Oh, my sweet Lemonade, they were both just broken to their core . . . their hearts shattered in so many pieces after Rebecca died that they didn't know how to fix it. And instead of holding on to each other through their grief with love and gratitude, their sadness came out in anger, and their anger tore them apart."

I don't know what to say about that, so I don't say anything. We sit for a spell while we sip and munch on egg salad fingers.

"I know how hard it's been for you," Mrs. Dickerson says quietly, smiling a crooked pink-lipsticked smile at me. "Life is the definition of loss. But it makes us grow, and it makes us stronger. The most important thing to remember is to have gratitude for those we love and those who love us. Even if it's not for the amount of time we expected or wished for. If you don't, you can be washed away by the sadness."

"You know what it feels like sometimes?" I ask. "Kind of like I have to carry something that's way too heavy, and I can't find any place to set it down. And it makes my whole body ache."

She nods slowly with her eyes closed.

"You may never find that place to put it down, but I promise you that the load will become lighter. And one day, you may even forget it's with you any longer, but it will be with you. Elizabeth will *always* be a part of you, making you stronger, braver, and more loving because of what you've carried. Your task now . . ."

She takes a long drink of her tea. "Your task is to learn to accept your new life without forgetting the gifts of your past. These are the gifts of your new life, Lemonade." She holds out her arms. "Willow Creek . . . Charlie . . . Tobin . . . Trust it. Embrace it. Be thankful for it."

I think hard about her words.

"I *am* thankful for Mama," I say. "And other things too."

"Like what?" she asks.

"You, for one," I say. "And your cookies, for another."

Mrs. Dickerson laughs until she wipes at the teardrops squeezing out the edges of her eyes. Black smudges appear on the white cloth napkin in her hand.

"Oh, Lemonade, you are so much like her. Do you know that?"

I wipe my tears too.

"I used to know it," I tell her. "But I think I might have forgotten."

# 23

# A NEW LIFE

After lunch at Mrs. Dickerson's, I head back to town. My stomach is full and my eyes are heavy after being up so late the night before. When I reach the library, I see the blue house. 1808.

Nick French's house.

There are kids running and hiding in the bushes. Laughing. Playing. Having fun.

Like they have no worries in their life.

No lava. No quicksand. No heavy loads to carry.

I keep walking, watching out of the corner of my eye. There are two girls pointing toward me and whispering. Some boys poke elbows at each other and laugh at me.

I pick up the pace.

"Hey!" someone calls. "San Fran!"

It's Buzz Cut.

"You playing?" he asks.

I stop in front of the driveway. Everyone is watching me now. Waiting for an answer.

I don't give them one.

"Come on!" a cute boy calls out to me. "We don't bite!"

Everyone laughs, and so do I.

He's even cuter than Craig Lundgren at Sherman Elementary. He has brown eyes and a wide smile stuck smack dab in the middle of two deep dimples on each cheek.

Then they all stand there looking at me, waiting for my answer.

"That's Jorge," Buzz Cut tells me, pointing to the cute boy. "But we just call him J-Man. And that's Eliza Rose and Mei Cunningham and Nick French. And you know Beau." He points a thumb at the kid with the bangs.

I look down the street toward Charlie's house. It would be a lot easier to hide under the rainbow comforter with my book than to stay. Or go back to manning the Bigfoot Headquarters, which is where I'm supposed to be anyhow.

I look at the girls again. They're still whispering about me. I wonder what they're saying.

I think about my friends back home and how much I miss them. Melanie, Lisa S., Angela K., and Shelley H. They were all so much fun.

And so was I . . . before.

I think about what Mrs. Dickerson said about accepting change. I think about the zesty girl in the round frame from the hall. And about what it used to mean to be Lemonade.

*Elizabeth Lilly Witt.*

"Well?" Buzz Cut says. "Are you going to just stand there all day or are you playing?"

"All right," I say, feeling a sudden pain in my stomach and wondering if it's appendicitis. "I'll play."

"Cool," he says.

I take a step toward the driveway.

One step toward my new life.

• • •

On my way home, I try to remember the names of all the kids I met.

Eliza Rose Cline is going into fourth grade, and her cat just had kittens, and she said I could have one if Charlie says it's okay.

Mei Cunningham, going into fifth grade like me. She's adopted from China and knows how to speak English *and* Chinese.

Jorge Santamaria may just be the cutest boy on the planet. And I found out, when we were both hiding behind a pine tree, that he loves Twinkies too! And he agrees that they are way better than Ho Hos, Ding Dongs, or even Banana Flips.

Nick French is real quiet and turns the color of maraschino cherries whenever Mei is around him, because he sent her a note asking if she wants to be his girlfriend, and Mei said yes. Now they don't talk or look at each other or anything.

I also found out Buzz Cut's real name is Joe Kelly. And Bangs is Beau Stitch.

All in all, it's a real fun day. Kick the Can is kind of like tag with a twist. The twist being that there isn't a can at all. The can is technically a dirty orange Nerf football. But to call it Kick the Dirty Orange Nerf Football sounds kind of lame, I guess.

I've never played Kick the Anything before.

And I liked it.

In the city, we roller-skate, play hopscotch on the sidewalk, or jump rope. And in the evening, sometimes the boys on Beacon will let us play baseball with them in the alley. Jimmy Libertine always lets me be catcher, even though I miss the ball more than I catch it. Erika Vass says it's 'cause he's in love with me, and maybe he is, because one time he gave me a whole bouquet of Tootsie Pops.

If Tootsie Pops equal love, I guess he loves me a whole bunch, because he gave me a full dozen. And they were all cherry, which everyone knows is the very best flavor of Tootsie Pop there is.

"Where have you been?" Tobin hollers at me from Charlie's front porch. He's pacing back and forth with the yellow legal pad tucked under his arm and a pencil stuck behind his ear.

"I, ah . . . I, um . . . ," I start.

It didn't occur to me that I needed to keep my afternoon a secret. I mean, it's not like I'm not allowed to play with other kids. But for some reason, right this minute, I can't make my mouth say the words.

"I was, um . . . out having tea and cookies with Mrs. Dickerson," I tell him.

Which isn't exactly a lie.

"Did she report another sighting?" he asks, sitting down on the porch swing.

"No," I say, making my way up the driveway. "I just wanted to hear some more stories about Mama."

"I counted on you to be in charge of the Bigfoot Headquarters, and you leave for the day?"

"What's the big deal?"

"The big deal is that I trusted you to be in charge for the very first time, and you went and had tea and cookies instead. *That's* the big deal. But I guess that doesn't matter to you. Nothing matters to you."

"What's that supposed to mean?"

"Nothing," he mumbles.

"Where's Charlie?" I ask.

"He's already inside starting dinner," Tobin says. "Because you weren't here for that, either."

"Lemonade," Charlie calls through the screen door. "Is that you?"

"Yes, Charlie," I call back.

"Miss Cotton is on the phone for you."

Tobin's brow lowers and his eyes stare hard at me.

"What's with you?" I ask.

"Nothing," he says, getting up off the swing and making his way down the porch steps.

"Where are you going?" I ask him.

He doesn't say one word.

I watch him cross the street, walk up his driveway, and pull open the screen door.

It slams behind him.

• • •

That night, after dinner and after my Irish Spring bath, I find Charlie in the living room watching *Barnaby Jones*.

"Charlie?"

"Yes?" He gets up from the couch with the big leaves on it and turns the volume down.

"I have a question for you," I say.

He sits back down and pats a leaf next to him, like I'm supposed to sit there.

"Well, let's hear it," he says.

I decide to slide one hip down onto a different leaf in the matching chair across the room instead.

"Where's Tobin's dad?" I ask.

Charlie breathes out slow and long, then folds his glasses and slips them into his shirt pocket.

"Lem, Scotty was drafted to go to Vietnam. Goodness, it was about five or so years ago now . . . and, well . . . he never came back home."

"Did he die?"

Charlie shakes his head.

"We don't know. Two military men came to the house about a year after he went in and told Debbie he was MIA. Missing in action. I think at that time, we all held out hope that he was still alive, but it became harder with each passing year."

"So, you think he *did* die, then?"

"Well, we feared that was the case, and then Debbie got a call last year from the army letting her know he was found."

"Then he *is* alive?"

"He was a prisoner of war for many years. Three total. That's a very long time to live like that. The prisoners were tortured in horrific ways. Debbie was told that Scotty was found and that he would be transported back to Oakland for a debriefing and then discharged home. They told her he was okay, but she didn't know exactly what condition he was in after all he had gone through."

"So he's still in Oakland?"

"We don't know."

I drop my chin in my hand and sigh.

"I guess I don't understand," I say.

"Debbie received a letter from Scotty when he made it back to California, letting her know how much he loved her and that he couldn't wait to get home to see her and Tobin. And then he was gone."

"What do you mean, gone? Where did he go?"

"What we know is that he was discharged from the army and then given an airline ticket home to Redding. But when Debbie and Tobin went to pick him up at the airport . . . he wasn't there. They found out he hadn't even made it on the plane."

"What do you think happened to him?"

"I don't know the answer to that," he says. "But what I *do* know is that Scotty loved his family more than anything in this world and something very bad must've happened to keep him from them."

I swallow hard.

"But they're still waiting for him? Tobin and his mom?" I ask.

"Yes, they hold out hope that he's okay. They love him very much."

I think about that.

"Do *you* think he could still come home?"

"I hope so, Lem," he says. "For their sake, I truly hope he does . . . but the sad truth is that we may never know what happened to him. There are still many missing soldiers out there even after the war has ended, and we just don't have the answers."

"Is that why Tobin is the way he is?"

"How's that?"

"You know . . . kind of . . . well, particular, really."

Charlie smiles.

"I think it's all in the way you look at it. I find him particularly . . . special. With elements of personality that few people share. Smart, funny, and full of questions that he needs answered. I think he's a very special kid."

"Oh, me too," I say. "But it would be nice to know other kids too."

"Well, of course it would. I certainly don't see anything wrong with that." Charlie strokes his beard and looks at me for a long moment. "What's this about, Lem?"

I take a deep breath and look at the furry pink slippers on my feet. The ones Mama gave me for Christmas last year.

"I played Kick the Can today at Nick French's house with some other kids," I say.

"Uh-huh," Charlie says. "I still don't see the problem."

"Well, I guess Tobin doesn't really fit in here."

"Ahhhh," Charlie says.

"Some even make fun of him," I say.

He pauses for a minute while he thinks about what he wants to say.

"Yes, he's had some struggles with kids his age."

"The two boys who came into the store the other day," I say. "Joe Kelly and Beau Stitch. They give Tobin a pretty hard time, and Joe is the one who invited me to play."

"I see."

"At first, I didn't think there was really anything wrong with it. At least that's what I told myself, but when I got home, I, ah, well, I lied to Tobin about where I'd been."

"Mmmm."

"I guess I didn't want to hurt his feelings."

"Yes, I see that." Charlie strokes his beard and thinks hard about my question. "Lem, one of the things that was really unique about your mother was that she got along with everyone. No matter who they were. She never judged anyone for being different or treated anyone unkindly because of who they were or what they'd been through."

"I'm the same way." I point to myself. "I mean, I used to be. At home I am. I have lots of friends. Erika is my very best friend. And there's Melanie, Lisa S., Angela K., and Shelley H.—" I start to list on my fingers.

"I don't doubt it," he says. "I don't doubt it. You are so much like her. Maybe this is an opportunity for you to help Tobin bridge a gap that he hasn't figured out how to bridge on his own just yet. I would think you're just the person to do it."

"So, you're saying you think I should tell him?"

"I think you should make those decisions on your own. I'm just saying you're so much like your mother that I forget sometimes that you are you. And one thing I know is that she would find a way to bring everyone together."

I think about it.

"Thanks, Charlie," I say.

"You're welcome, Lem. I hope I helped."

I smile.

"You did."

# 24

# MR. HAROLD'S RANCH

Tobin isn't at breakfast the next morning.

Charlie and I eat our daily bowls of sticks and seeds and bark without him. After Charlie leaves for the store, I head to the beat-up garage, aka the Bigfoot Headquarters, to report for my daily shift. Tobin is already at the desk.

"Hi," I say to him.

He's furiously scribbling in his yellow legal pad.

"Hello?" I say. *"Ni hao?"*

Mei Cunningham taught me three of the most important phrases to know in the Chinese language:

Hello

Good-bye

Where's the bathroom?

Tobin looks up at me like he hasn't heard a thing I've said.

"We've got a major sighting. *Major* sighting!"

"I hope she made the gingersnaps today," I say. "They're my favorite."

"It's not Mrs. Dickerson," he says.

"Who, then?"

"We've got to go right now. One was just spotted. Come on." He grabs his leather case. "I'll tell you on the way."

* * *

Tobin pedals furiously while I white-knuckle the handlebars and keep my mouth closed up tight.

"Lester Harold has a ranch on the east side of town. He called to say he saw a Bigfoot crouched in the woods just past the fence around his pasture," Tobin hollers in my ear as he pumps the pedals. "Not more than ten minutes ago. He swears it was at least nine feet tall!"

He makes a sharp right, and I move left to balance my weight. I've gotten pretty good at riding on Tobin's handlebars, and I'm not quite as scared as I was. I can even keep my eyes open the whole time now.

It's the words *nine feet tall* that make me break my own rule, and I open my mouth to holler back at him.

"Nine feet tall? That can't be right."

"Oh, it's right, all right," Tobin says.

My heart is pounding in my chest. I can feel it in my neck and inside my ears, too.

*Nine* feet? If Mr. Harold is right about that, it sure is reason to believe it's no man in a costume putting one over on him. What man is that tall?

Tobin keeps pumping over paved streets and unpaved

bumpy roads until he turns at a black iron gate with curly letters on it.

Harold Ranch
Homestead
1924

There's a mailbox on the side of the dirt drive with the number 45018. Tobin pumps his pedals up the long driveway. There are black cows on both sides, fenced in behind weathered wood and barbed wire.

They stare at us, slowly chewing on the tall grass from the pasture. They stare and chew and chew and stare.

"I wonder what cows think about," I say.

"They're steers," Tobin says.

"What?"

"They're steers, not cows."

"They look like cows to me."

"Well, they're not. They're steers."

"What's the difference?"

"How should I know the difference? I'm not a rancher."

"Then how do you know for sure they're not cows?"

"I just know."

"That seems pretty unscientific, if you ask me."

He heaves a good, long sigh, letting me know he's done answering my questions about cows or steers. At the end of the long dirt drive, there's a big white farmhouse with a small front porch. Off to the left is a bright red barn with white trim. Chickens squawk at us as Tobin pedals through a pack of five or six of them roaming free. Tobin stops his bike in front of the house next to an old blue Ford pickup with bales of hay loaded in the back.

I start sneezing right away.

"Great!" Tobin rolls his eyes at me while he unties his black case from the back of his bike.

"It's not like I'm doing it on purpose." I wipe my nose.

I guess I'm allergic to more than just expeditions.

The screen door slams, and a tall man in worn overalls steps onto the porch. He has on a yellowing T-shirt with wet patches on the chest and under the arms. His gray hair is thin enough that you can see his head through the strands, which are slicked flat. He pulls a red handkerchief from the bib pocket of his overalls and wipes it across the back of his neck.

"Mr. Harold!" Tobin calls, walking toward him with an outstretched hand. "Thank you for trusting Bigfoot Detectives Inc. with your Bigfoot needs."

Mr. Harold grabs Tobin's hand and gives it a strong shake.

"I'm glad you could make it out so fast. I can't believe I saw what I saw, you know? It's just too unbelievable. I mean, I hear all the talk, you know, but I didn't really believe it . . . not really, I didn't." Then he looks at me. "Until I saw it with my own eyes."

I swallow hard.

"Yes, sir," Tobin says. "Mr. Harold, this is my assistant, Lemonade Liberty Witt."

"Pleasure." Mr. Harold reaches a hand out to me.

It's dark and tan and rough with brown spots on top. He wraps his long fingers around mine with a sturdy shake.

"Heard you were staying with Charlie," he says. "Welcome to Willow Creek. Glad to have you here."

"Thank you," I say.

"Tell us again exactly what you saw." Tobin pulls his yellow legal pad and a Bic pen out of his leather case to take notes. "Every detail you can remember."

"Please." Mr. Harold motions for us to sit with him on the porch steps.

Tobin sits on the top step next to Mr. Harold, and I sit two steps below Tobin.

"I still can't believe it." Mr. Harold breathes, wiping the back of his neck again, looking far off into the pasture.

"Take your time, Mr. Harold," Tobin says. "Don't leave anything out."

Mr. Harold bobs his head once.

"I was in the field on my horse, Cimarron," he says. "There's a forest on the west side of the pasture. Thick, too. Goes on for miles. So, I set to fixing a portion of the fence. That's when I saw him."

"What exactly did you see?" I ask.

Mr. Harold looks at me.

"Bigfoot," he says matter-of-factly.

"Are you sure, Mr. Harold?" I ask.

"I can tell you this, there isn't a question in my mind that that's what I saw."

I swallow hard again.

"What did he look like?" Tobin asks, scribbling on his pad. "Every detail, Mr. Harold, don't leave *anything* out."

"Well, he was big. At least three feet taller than me, and I'm six-five. I got off Cimarron and was gathering up my tools to fix the fence post, and that's when I felt the first rock hit me."

"He threw rocks," Tobin says.

"Yep. I felt the first one hit my arm, and when I looked up, there he was, crouched near a tree. Our eyes met. Then I watched him throw another one. This one nearly got me in the forehead, but I ducked in time. Then he growled this incredible growl that I swear made the ground shake underneath me."

"And then what happened?" I breathe.

"Then he ran off into the woods. Fast as anything else wild that I've seen traverse that ground back in there."

"The midtarsal break," I say.

"Exactly," Tobin says.

Mr. Harold looks confused. "The what?"

"Never mind, Mr. Harold. Nine feet, you think?" Tobin asks.

"I'm sure of it," Mr. Harold says.

"What color was it?" Tobin asks.

"It had reddish-brown hair. Long, too."

"Could it have been a bear, Mr. Harold?" I ask him. "A bear on his hind legs?"

I can hear Tobin huff air out, and I feel him giving me a good glare.

"A bear with opposable thumbs?" Tobin says sarcastically. "You need opposable thumbs to throw rocks, you know."

"It's okay. That's a fair question, Lemonade." Mr. Harold turns to me. "I would ask the same thing if I hadn't seen it with my own eyes."

"How do you know for sure it was a Bigfoot, is what I'm asking, Mr. Harold?"

"It was close. I mean real close. I suppose that's why he threw the rocks. He got scared seeing me near him like that. Anyway, that thing was closer than I ever want to see it again. And let me tell you, I saw everything. And I know it wasn't a bear."

"What about a man in a costume?"

"Lemonade!" Tobin hollers.

"It's okay, Tobin," Mr. Harold says. "I think a true scientist has to rule out everything. Those questions are all questions I asked myself."

"And what did you answer yourself?" I ask.

"It wasn't a bear. It wasn't a costume. It was real. Really real. It was a Bigfoot. It was an animal for sure, and none I've ever seen before."

"But what makes you so absolutely sure you saw what you think you saw?" I ask.

"We were eye to eye. I saw his facial features. There was skin and hair and brown eyes. It wasn't a mask. And when he stood up to throw that rock and then run, I could make out the muscles underneath his coat of fur. Large muscles you could see with every movement."

"Wow," Tobin breathes, frantically scribbling on his yellow pad.

"And there was this smell, too . . ." Mr. Harold stares off in the direction of the pasture again.

"Skunk?" Tobin asks.

"Exactly right. At first I thought there must have been a

skunk somewhere near, but it was him. When he ran off, I knew it was him."

"Were you scared, Mr. Harold?" I ask.

"Yes, I was scared. I'm not going to lie. I was scared because he was scared, and you never know what an animal will do when it's acting on fear alone."

"Yes, sir," I tell him.

"And he was big, too. Bigger than any bear I've ever seen."

"Mr. Harold," Tobin says. "Can you remember anything else? Anything else you might have left out?"

"His face had a wrinkled nose, kind of like a chimp or gorilla might have, with that same reddish hair on his face and the same color skin. Reddish brown . . . and there's one more thing I can say for absolute sure . . ."

Tobin looks up from his pad.

"Yes?"

Mr. Harold leans in close to us.

"He wasn't alone."

• • •

"That's an incredible sighting!" Charlie exclaims from his stool behind the counter when we get to Bigfoot Souvenirs and More. "Did you find any prints or hair evidence?"

"No," Tobin says. "We searched just past the fence where he said he saw it, but we didn't find anything. There was more grass than dirt or mud. We didn't see any prints or hair or scat. But Mr. Harold gave us this." Tobin holds his hand out toward Charlie.

"A rock?" Charlie asks, taking it.

"Not just *any* rock. One of the rocks that the Bigfoot threw at him!" Tobin exclaims.

"Amazing," Charlie breathes, holding the rock tight.

"Here's the thing, though," I say. "After he gave us all the details about what he looked like . . . Mr. Harold said one more very important thing."

"And what was that?" Charlie asks.

"He said the Bigfoot wasn't alone."

"Mmmm," Charlie says, leaning back on his stool. "Did he elaborate?"

"He said he knew for sure there were others just beyond in the woods . . . watching."

Charlie raises his eyebrows.

"A family?" Tobin says.

We stare at each other with wide eyes.

"I think we should plan an expedition at Mr. Harold's farm tonight!" I point my finger in the air and jump up and down. "Can we, Charlie? Can we?"

Charlie chuckles from deep inside his belly.

"Well, look at you." He smiles down at me. "Tobin, it looks like we're going to make Lem a Bigfoot enthusiast after all. Maybe we'll even convince her to stay." He winks.

I think about it.

And it's actually the first time I don't want to tell them *"Fat chance."*

# 25

# OPERATION:
# THE HAROLD RANCH EXPEDITION

A camp-out in Mr. Harold's backyard that evening is the closest thing to an expedition that Charlie and Debbie agree to let us do on our own in the dark. Which Tobin grumbles about the whole time they're setting up the tent.

"I'm sorry, Tobin," Debbie says, pounding in a stake. "It's just not safe to be in the woods alone all night."

"I won't be alone. I have Lemonade."

"Yes, you do!" Charlie smiles, tying a cord to a stake already in the ground. "Yes, you do!"

"Mr. Harold, is it okay if we use your bathroom instead of the woods tonight?" I ask.

"Of course. The door will be open, so you just help yourself to whatever you need. There are extra blankets if you get cold, and of course if it rains, you two just come right on inside."

"Now, is there anything else I can do before I leave?" Charlie asks, double-tying the final cord to the ground.

"Nope," Tobin says.

"Okay, well, I packed granola bars and juice for you both, and some extra Twinkies for Lem." He hands me a brown paper bag.

"Thank you, Charlie." Debbie smiles at him and puts a hand on his arm.

"Who has time to eat when cryptozoological discovery is about to be made? All we really need is this." Tobin holds up his movie camera. "I think tonight is the night. I can feel it! Lemonade, tonight we make history!"

"Good luck, kids. I'll be back to pick you up in the morning."

We wave good-bye to Jake as Charlie and Debbie drive down the long dirt drive into the setting sun. The sky is a brilliant orange with a few gray clouds in the distance. But no matter how dark those few clouds are, they can't block out the bright pinks and warm reds and fiery oranges that stretch across the sky as the sun finds its way behind the pines. A cooling breeze blows, moving my hair off my shoulders and making chicken skin sprout up on my arms.

I look at the clouds way off in the distance one more time, hoping they stay right where they are.

"I'll be in the house," Mr. Harold says. "The windows are open, so if you need me, you just holler. And again, if it starts to rain, you just come on inside. It looks like something might be coming."

"Yes, sir," Tobin says.

"Good night, then," Mr. Harold says.

"Night," we say together.

Tobin and I head to the tent and crawl inside. I find my wool jacket and sweatpants in my duffel bag and pull them on over my shorts and T-shirt.

"I'm staying up *all* night," Tobin informs me, sitting cross-legged on top of his sleeping bag. "Here, you're assigned to the still pictures on this mission."

He hands me the Polaroid camera. I sit down cross-legged on my sleeping bag facing him and slip the strap around my neck. We sit there staring at each other.

No one says anything.

"What do we do now?" I ask him.

"Wait," he says.

"For what?"

He leans forward and whispers then. "You'll know when you hear it."

"Oh," I say.

We wait.

There's a low, far-off rumble in the sky, and I take a deep breath. I hope Mr. Harold is wrong about something heading in this direction.

"Want to play Twenty Questions?" I ask.

"What's that?"

"You think of something, and you tell me if it's a person, place, or thing, and I have to guess it in twenty questions, and all you can answer is yes or no."

He shrugs. "Okay."

"You go first," I say.

Tobin smiles. "Ummm, okay, got something."

"You're thinking of something?"

"Yep," he says.

"You have to tell me if it's a person, place, or thing," I tell him.

"What if it's none of those?"

"What do you mean? It has to be one of those."

"Well, it's not."

I look at him and cock my head to one side.

"It's Bigfoot, isn't it?"

Tobin smiles even wider.

"You're so predictable," I tell him.

• • •

"Lem!"

"What? What is it?" I pop my head up.

Tobin rubs his eyes. "You fell asleep."

"You fell asleep first," I say.

"No . . . No . . . I wasn't sleeping, I was . . . I was . . . wait, what time is it?" He checks his Bigfoot watch. "Oh three hundred hours."

That's really three in the morning. Tiny taps of rain are hitting the top of the tent.

"It'll be light in a few hours," I say.

He nods.

I yawn. "I guess we're not going to get anything this time either."

"Not stuck in this tent, we won't," he says. "Unless . . ."

"Unless what?"

"Unless we *make* something happen."

"We aren't supposed to do that," I say. "Charlie and Debbie said to stay in the yard."

"We will, but there's no harm in exploring closer to the fence post out in the west end of the pasture."

"The pasture's not the yard. They said to stay in the yard. Plus, it's storming out," I say.

He holds one palm outside the tent flap. "It's barely a drizzle," he says. "Anyway, pasture, yard . . . what's the difference?"

"There's a big difference," I tell him. "That's why they said to stay in the yard."

"If you're too chicken, I can go by myself."

"I'm not chicken," I insist.

"Sounds *fowl* to me."

"Okay," I agree. "But if it starts storming, I'm going inside."

"Fine," Tobin says. "Let's synchronize."

"You know I don't have a watch."

"The cameras," he says.

"Oh."

"Cameras ready?" he asks.

"Check," I say.

"Check," he says.

"This might be our night, Lemonade Liberty Witt."

"Is it coming down harder?" I ask.

"Quit being a chicken, it's just a little—"

And it's just then that we hear this horrible sound. A long, high-pitched howl from the woods.

"Whoooooooooooooo!"

I grab his arm. "What's that?"

My heart pounds hard in my chest, and the wool jacket and sweatpants suddenly make me feel like I'm wearing a snowsuit in a sauna.

"I knew it!" Tobin exclaims. "It's them! They're here! They're *here*! Let's go!"

# 26

# SLOPPY DROPS MAKE
# FOR REAL MUSHY COW PIES

Mr. Harold's pasture starts just past the barn. It goes on forever and is filled with steers, trees, and grass for grazing. There's a wooden fence keeping everything from getting out.

Except for a free-roaming Tobin.

"Wait for me!" I call after him.

I can barely make him out in the dark as he runs ahead of me straight for the west end of the pasture.

"Hurry up!" he whispers back at me. "And would you be quiet?"

"I'm going as fast as I can!"

It's hard to run with a Polaroid camera around your neck and sweatpants over your shorts. It's even harder to do those things while dodging disgusting, smelly cow pies.

Or maybe they're called steer pies.

The mini stinky land mines are all over the pasture. And since it's rainy, they're *slippery* stinky land mines. In the dark, dodging them is practically impossible. Each time my tennis shoe hits one, I feel it splat back up on my ankle, and I lose my balance a little.

Black steers stand in groups under the pouring rain, staring at us as we run by them.

Still chewing. Probably laughing at us slipping and sliding through their poo.

Tobin is getting farther and farther away from me, and the rain is coming down harder.

"Wait up!" I demand.

"Shhh!" he hisses back at me. "Mr. Harold is going to hear you!"

I stop to catch my breath. Squinting through the drops, I see something catapulting over the wooden fence at the end of the pasture.

"You're not supposed to go past the fence!" I holler at him through cupped hands, not caring if Mr. Harold hears me or not.

"Tobin!" I scream with all that's in me. "Tobin!"

He's gone.

And that's when it happens again. A long, high-pitched howl from the woods.

"Whooooooooooooo!"

My heart jumps and I start to run again. Harder. Pushing through the downpour to get to him. Rain and tears make rivers down my cheeks until I get to the fence.

"Tobin! Where are you?"

Nothing.

"Tobin!"

"Here! Over here!" His voice finds me from inside the forest past the fence.

The raindrops are so thick now, and sloppy, too. More like freezing buckets of water instead of tiny drips. They hit me on my forehead and my cheeks, sometimes plopping right into my eyes, making it hard to see anything at all. I push the hair out of my face and wipe at my eyes with my wet jacket sleeve, which now feels like a sopping sponge.

There's a flash of light and then a low roll of thunder. I don't even have time to count to see how far away it is—the storm is right on top of us. I want to run back to the tent and hide in the thick, warm sleeping bag. I want to run inside, where I know Mr. Harold has warm blankets somewhere and maybe even a cozy pullout couch.

The wood of the fence is wet and slippery, and so is the tall grass. When I pull myself over the fence, I slip and fall onto the other side.

"Tobin!" I yell again, pushing myself up from the mud.

I don't hear anything this time. Nothing but the rain cutting through the leaves and grass. It's coming down fast and hard now, with crashing thunder and bright flashes across the sky.

"Tobin!" I cry. "Where are you?"

I crouch down under a tall pine and crawl underneath the lowest branch. I wait, wiping at my eyes again with my soaked jacket.

"Mama," I whisper. "I'm so scared, Mama."

A crash right overhead shakes the needles on the branches above me. I cover my ears with my hands.

*Elizabeth Lilly Witt.*

More thunder, and then a blinding flash lights the forest for a count of two seconds.

I know I'm going to be lost in these woods. I'll drown in the drops and they'll find my frozen body at daybreak. Or I'll be electrocuted by lightning. Or the wind will blow this pine down on top of me and I'll be squished to death.

"What a shame," Mrs. Dickerson will say. "She was so young. And just the spitting image of her mother, too."

I shiver and my teeth chatter. I wipe at my eyes again with my wet jacket.

To the left, I hear a rustling in the brush that's too big to be the wind.

Then heavy footsteps pounding the damp ground.

Please be Tobin.

Please be Tobin.

Please be Tobin.

I squeeze my eyes closed, praying inside my head.

Closer.

The footsteps are too heavy to be his. I know it. I can feel them vibrate underneath me as they pound the mud. I duck my head even lower under the pine branch.

Closer.

Pound.

Pound.

Pound.

They hit the earth, sloshing soggy grass and sticks underneath them.

Closer.

It's what nine feet tall sounds like, I know it. And then the branch I'm hiding under moves, and I scream.

"Lemonade!"

I open my eyes to see Mr. Harold standing above me in a shiny black rain slicker and big black rubber boots.

"What are you doing out here? Where's Tobin?"

I start to sob.

"I—I don't know."

## 27

# CRUEL AND UNUSUAL

We're in big trouble.

I mean *trouble*.

Like trouble with a capital *T* and an exclamation point at the end.

"What were you *thinking*?"

That's from Debbie, once the sun comes up that morning. She's still wearing her pajamas and a matching robe with little yellow flowers on it. Her hair is all messed up, she has black mascara smudged under her eyes, and there's more red around the rims than normal. Tobin and Charlie and I are all sitting around Charlie's kitchen table, while Debbie paces the floor.

Back and forth.

"Mom," Tobin protests. "You don't understand. They were howling! I'm a scientist. What choice did I have, really?"

"I don't care if they were performing the two-step to 'When the Saints Come Marching In,'" she tells him with her hands on her hips.

Tobin looks at me, confused.

"Two-step? Mom, the Bigfoot have opposable thumbs, but I'm fairly sure they can't dance the—"

"Tobin!"

"Yes, ma'am," he says, looking at his shoes.

"We care about you," she goes on. "About Lemonade. We care about your safety. That's why we set rules."

"Yes, ma'am," he says again.

Charlie is stroking his beard and looking out the window while he silently sips his coffee.

"There were rules," Tobin's mom goes on. "Rules for a reason, and you didn't follow them."

"I'm sorry, Debbie," I say.

"Me too," Tobin says. "We promise we won't go past the fence next time."

"Next time?" Tobin's mom says with a snort that sounds like a laugh but really isn't one. "There won't be a next time, young man. You're grounded. And no going to the Bigfoot Headquarters for one week."

"A whole week!" Tobin shouts desperately, standing straight up. "What about the neighbors? The sightings? Mrs. Dickerson? They *need* us."

"They'll have to find a way to get along without you. Right, Charlie?"

Charlie looks at Debbie, nods slowly, and then takes another long drink from his mug.

"I could use some help at the store this week," he says quietly. "I have some shipments coming in. You can both spend the week there."

"It's settled, then." Debbie bobs her head down like she's putting a period at the end of a thought. "I don't ever want to go through this again."

"You won't, Debbie," I say. "We promise. Right, Tobin?"

"In the name of Bigfoot science, I find this punishment cruel and unusual for the following reasons—" he starts, holding out his fingers to make the list.

I poke him hard with my elbow.

"Ow," he mumbles, then sits back down in his chair and folds his arms.

"Tobin?" Debbie says again. "I hope we understand each other."

"Yeah, okay," he says with his chin on his chest.

• • •

After a hot, bubble-less bath with the same old boring bar of Irish Spring and a plain blue washcloth, I spend the rest of Sunday afternoon in my room. Another penalty doled out during the judgment phase of our kitchen table trial.

I reread all the letters from San Francisco five times each. I have eight now. Two more from Erika Vass and one from Shelley H. and one from Melanie, too. Erika had her summer dance recital and Melanie's mom had the baby. It was a girl. Melanie says it screams all night long so she's started wearing cotton balls in her ears.

While I'm rereading Miss Cotton's letters, Charlie

knocks softly on the door. I slip the letters in the drawer of the night table.

"Come in," I call.

Charlie comes in and sits down next to me. He hands me a book.

"I ordered this for you at the store."

I look it over, front and back.

"Thanks, Charlie," I say.

"It's supposed to be a good one for a girl your age," he says.

It has a cat and a mouse on the cover, and it's called *The Cricket in Times Square*.

"I love cats," I tell him.

"I also want you to know that when I lay down rules, I expect you to follow them."

"Yes, Charlie."

"The rules aren't to ruin your fun. They are for your safety and what I think is best for you."

"I know it," I say, feeling the lump coming up in my throat. "And I really am sorry."

I want to tell him it was all Tobin's fault anyway. He was the one who had to go running into the woods after that thing in the pouring rain. All I wanted to do was make a break for the house and hide under a warm blanket until the thunder stopped rumbling.

But I don't tell Charlie any of it.

Mostly because it would make me sound like a big fat chicken.

"It won't ever happen again," I promise him.

"I hope not," he says.

. . .

I fold down page fifty-five of my book and go to the bedroom door to listen. After hearing the faint sounds of the news on the television in the living room, I tiptoe over to the big trunk at the end of the bed. I wrap my fingers around the edges and inch the top up little by little. It gripes and groans until it finally gives way.

I stop and take a deep breath before I push the lid all the way up and back against the bed. I stare at all the carefully folded piles, afraid to touch anything.

Children's clothes, toys, games, and stuffed animals carefully placed in perfect rows. The cedar escapes into the room and penetrates the air.

I know they're hers.

I know it without even asking the question.

The lump starts up in my throat again, and I quickly close the lid. Making sure it's shut tight so the memories don't escape, and so the sadness stuck in my throat can't suck me into the quicksand.

Sadness quicksand that's deep and scary.

So deep and scary that I'm afraid one day I won't be able to come back from it.

# 28

# THE RETURN OF
# DELORES JAWORSKI

We finally make it to Friday.

The very last day of our sentence.

It's not as bad as I thought it would be. I've actually had fun hanging out with Charlie at the store all week. He even taught me how to ring up customers on the cash register. I have to stand on the step stool to reach it, but still, I feel very grown-up doing it.

Today, though, is our very last day, and our official parole starts at exactly 1700 hours, which is really five o'clock, which is exactly the time when Charlie locks the green door at Bigfoot Souvenirs and More.

Until that time, and not a minute sooner, I'm assigned to EXOTIC JERKIES OF THE WORLD, unpacking and sorting and stocking. Charlie just added wild boar and Tibetan yak to his already-disgusting collection of shriveled-up meat in a bag.

The bell on the door rings.

"Good morning!" Charlie calls, like he always does to every single solitary person who passes through that green door. But this morning his voice sounds weird on the last word.

Tight.

He clears his throat.

"Hello, Delores," he says, and clears his throat again. "Lem," he calls to me.

I pop my head up and peek between FINE CUISINE and BIGFOOT SCHOOL SUPPLIES.

It's her.

Delores Jaworski. The one who drove me here from San Francisco. The one I beat at the alphabet game when I spotted the Q on a liquor store outside Redding.

I wonder if she remembered to bring an order of Mr. Chin's fried egg rolls like I asked her to.

I set down the packages of jerky and step up to the front counter, where Charlie has been busy doing his accounting work in a green spiral notebook.

"You remember Miss Jaworski?" Charlie nods in her direction, his lips stuck on his teeth like he brushed them with Super Glue instead of the Colgate in the bathroom drawer.

"Yes, hello," I say.

"Good morning, Lemonade." She smiles warmly, holding her hand out to me.

I take her hand in mine, and she shakes it softly. Her fingers are bony and cold. She looks like the women do in San Francisco in her fancy red dress with black polka dots and black high heels. Her hair is twisted in a tight knot at the back of her neck, and she has on crisp red lipstick that knows exactly where it's supposed to be and stays there. All she has in her other hand is a bunch of papers and a large envelope.

She must have forgotten the egg rolls.

"I came to check up on you and see how things are going here," she says.

"Oh," I say, looking at Charlie.

"Things are going just fine here," Charlie tells her, his lips still glued against his teeth.

"You're working in the store?" She looks at Charlie with confusion. "Do you earn money for that?"

"No, we're being punished—" I start.

"We, ah . . ." Charlie clears his throat. "We had, ah, just a bit of a mishap, and the kids are helping out in the store as a consequence."

"Oh?" She looks back at me.

"In our defense," Tobin calls from the high ladder where he's dusting the wooden Bigfoot with a feather duster, "it was in the name of cryptozoological research, which makes the offense highly debatable."

I laugh nervously.

"That's Tobin," I tell her.

She smiles. "A friend of yours?"

"Yes," I say, looking back at him. "He is my friend."

"Tobin," Charlie calls. "Come and say hello to Miss Jaworski."

Tobin hops off the ladder and walks up to the counter, twirling the feather duster with one hand.

"*Bigfoot Detectives Inc.*," Delores reads off his safari hat, as always strapped tight under his chin.

"That's right." He digs his card out of his khaki shorts. "I handle any and all of Willow Creek's Bigfoot needs. Well, me and Lemonade now."

### BIGFOOT DETECTIVES INC.
Handling all your Bigfoot needs since 1974
Tobin Sky: 555-0906
And Lemonade Liberty Witt, Assistant

She examines the card.

"He needs that back," I tell her. "It's his only one."

"Oh." She smiles again, handing it back to Tobin. "Here you go. It's so nice to meet you. And Lemonade, I see you're getting used to Willow Creek after all."

"She's my assistant," Tobin says.

"Yes, I saw that on your, ah, card there."

He slips it back into his pocket.

"Well, I will get right to the point of my visit," Miss Jaworski tells Charlie.

"Please." Charlie motions to a stool near the counter.

"Thank you," she says, sliding onto the edge of the stool. "This was all a very sudden arrangement and somewhat temporary at the time we made plans. However, now someone has come forward to request guardianship of Lemonade."

Charlie doesn't say anything, his lips slowly slipping off his teeth.

"What does that mean?" Tobin asks, looking at me.

"I—I don't—" I start.

"Well, an option has come up, and I'm here to talk with Lemonade about that," Delores Jaworski tells Tobin.

"Who is making the request?" Charlie asks.

"Mary Cotton, Lemonade's fourth-grade teacher," she says, then turns to me. "She completed the paperwork, Lem. She would like you to come and live with her permanently."

"She did that?" I ask.

"Yes, honey, she sure did. She's put in a formal request to have a home study done to make sure she's suitable, which I'm sure she will be. So I'm here to let you know the request has been made and to talk about what our next steps might be."

"And what if I feel it's in Lem's best interest to stay here with us in Willow Creek?" Charlie asks, pressing his lips into a tight line.

"Oh . . . well, of course you are her legal guardian and her only living relative, so it's absolutely appropriate for her to remain here if you think that's in her best interest. However, Miss Cotton would be a wonderful guardian for Lem, and this option would allow Lem to return home."

*Home?*

"And . . . due to her age, Lem's opinion should also be considered in the decision. That being said, I guess . . . I mean, from what I understood, she has already made her decision. She told me she wanted to stay in San Francisco with all her friends and remain in the same school. And now she can—"

"Well, maybe she's changed her mind," Tobin interrupts, his voice getting louder.

Delores Jaworski turns to me, leaning down so we're eye to eye.

"Lemonade, how are you feeling about living here in Willow Creek with your grandfather?"

*Grandfather*.

"She can't leave!" Tobin exclaims before I even have a chance to open my mouth. "We're too close to making Bigfoot history. She can't leave. . . . I—I *need* her."

Then he turns to me.

"Tell her you're not leaving," he insists, his eyes getting red around the edges. "Tell her!"

## 29

# PAROLED

When Charlie locks the green door at Bigfoot Souvenirs and More, Tobin and I are finally sprung, our sentences complete. But it isn't the celebration I expected it to be.

"What are you so mad about? I didn't tell her I wanted to go," I say to Tobin in the backseat of Jake on the way home.

"You didn't say you wanted to stay." He points an accusing finger in my direction.

He's got me there.

Charlie's been especially quiet since Delores Jaworski left a manila envelope of papers on the counter before heading back to the city.

"And you've said all along that you're leaving here one day, right? Isn't that what you've said? Blowing this fruit stand?"

"Popsicle stand. It's a Popsicle stand," I remind him.

"And now here it is! The perfect opportunity for you to go back to your precious life in the city." Tobin stares out the window.

"I told you, I didn't say I wanted to go."

"Well, you didn't tell her you wanted to stay. I'm sorry I ever even made you my assistant."

"Is that right? Well, I'm the one who found the prints to begin with. If it wasn't for me, you'd have nothing."

"Stopping in the middle of an expedition to hog down another Twinkie and then stumbling onto prints doesn't give you any bragging rights, let me tell you. You would never even have *heard* of Bluff Creek if it hadn't been for me."

"Maybe if you'd made me partner to begin with, it would have given me a reason to stay," I say.

He turns his head from the window to face me.

"Does that mean if I promote you now, you'll stay?"

I think about it. He waits. I see Charlie glance at me in the rearview mirror, waiting for an answer too.

Everyone is waiting for an answer.

Even Delores Jaworski, who's on her way home to San Francisco.

But I don't have one.

"See!" Tobin sighs loudly, shifting in his seat and staring out the window again. "Just like I said."

Charlie's eyes are on the road again.

I lay my head on the back of the seat and watch the blurry solid white line along the edge of the highway.

*Elizabeth Lilly Witt.*

Why did you have to leave me?

## 30

# THE TRUNK

That night I can't sleep.

It feels like everyone in the world is mad at me. Like everyone in the world hates me.

I turn over and look at the clock. It's after two in the morning.

At home, when I couldn't sleep, Mama would get up and make us warm, bubbly milk on the stove that we would sip from big mugs at the kitchen table, and then she'd let me crawl into bed with her.

Miss Cotton would probably do that too.

It would be nice to be back home. I could go back to dance class with Erika Vass and start back up in Girl Scouts, which meets every Thursday at Melanie's house. I almost have enough credits to earn my Junior First Aid Badge.

I flip onto my right side, then onto my left, but I just can't get comfortable. I fluff the pillow and readjust one more

time. The bed feels harder than the ground did on both expeditions put together.

I reach over to click on the lamp next to my bed. I stare at
the trunk, then push the covers back and crawl over to it. I
put my hands flat on the lid and press my nose to it.

Cedar chips and musty wood.

I start on the lid again, pulling it upward as hard as I can,
trying not to make any noise. When it finally wiggles free, I
lift it all the way up and back against the bed.

I stare inside.

One by one, I pull out every last item in the trunk. The
baby clothes, perfectly folded and yellowing with age, a pair
of metal roller skates, a tarnished silver rattle, the Elvis
Presley concert T-shirt from the show that Mama and Debbie saw in the city, a pair of used-to-be-white baby shoes,
and a small box with red and blue and yellow ribbons for
first place, second, and third in track and field, softball, and
dance. Each item placed inside with special care. Each item
holding another story about Mama.

I pull out one treasured memory after another. Until I get
to the very bottom, where I see an old stuffed blue bunny
that's seen better days.

Its fur is gone in some spots, with only bare threads keeping it from bleeding out its stuffing. It's wearing a battered
pink ribbon around its neck.

I breathe the bunny in deep. Hoping it might still smell
like Mama. Like the disinfectant soap she washes her hands
with at work, Suave strawberry shampoo, and her Avon per-
fume all mixed together.

But all the bunny smells like is musty trunk and cedar.

She's gone.

Gone from me and gone from the trunk, too. Far from the memories stored away inside. I hold the bunny close and breathe in the cedar.

When the tears start to roll down my face, it's just one, then it's two, and then it's too many to count. I can't breathe. It feels like I'm never going to breathe again, like the tears are never going to stop.

I'm drowning.

Sinking in sadness quicksand.

And no one will ever find me.

"Mama!" I cry into the bunny's matted fur. "I don't know how to be here without you. I need you back, Mama. Please tell me what to do."

The bedroom doorknob turns, and the door creaks open. I scramble to my feet, wiping my face and hiding the blue bunny behind my back. Charlie, in his plaid pajamas and suede slippers, stares down at me. He glances around the floor at the messy piles of clothes, toys, and ribbons.

I brace myself for the yelling. The judgment. A new sentence.

I wait for it, wiping more tears and trying to find my breath.

"Can't sleep either, huh?" Charlie asks softly.

I shake my head.

"Hard day," he says, like it's a fact instead of a question.

I try my best to swallow the lump down, but it's so big now it feels like it won't ever go down again.

"When your mom was your age and she couldn't sleep, we used to heat up some milk together."

I wipe my nose across the length of my forearm.

"You did that?" I ask.

"Yes," he says.

"Together?"

He nods. "You can bring Rainbow if you like."

"Who?"

He juts a chin toward the blue bunny behind me. "That's what she called her."

I stare down at the floppy blue stuffed animal in my hands.

"How 'bout it? A mug of warm milk?"

I look back up at him.

"I'd like that," I say.

He holds out a hand toward me. A big hand. Rough, with straight nails and one very special silver ring. The hand is strong and tough, but kind.

A hand saving me from sinking in the quicksand. I guess there *is* someone looking out for me, making sure I don't drown.

Charlie.

"Ready?" he asks.

"Yes," I tell him, and slip my hand into his.

# 31

## GOING DOWN IN HISTORY

Tobin is a no-show for breakfast again the next morning. This time my stomach feels all twisted up inside about it too. And after I finish my sticks and seeds and bark, the twisting gets worse, and then the sweating starts, and I feel like I might even throw up.

Before I leave for the Bigfoot Headquarters, I set Rainbow right on top of my pillow. Then I pin my name badge to the front of my shirt. It's hot in the garage this morning, and I find Tobin sitting at the desk with the green receiver in his hand.

He doesn't look at me when I open the door.

"Yes, Mrs. Dickerson . . . uh-huh . . . There just never seem to be tracks or prints or anything we can measure. We're scientists, Mrs. Dickerson. We need concrete proof that—"

Pause.

"Uh-huh . . . yes, but . . . Okay, Mrs. Dickerson, we'll come out and check it out. Yes, ma'am . . . okay . . . good-bye."

He hangs up the phone and starts writing on his yellow legal pad.

"Another sighting at Mrs. Dickerson's?" I ask.

Nothing.

"You still mad?"

"I'm not mad," he says.

"Seems like you're mad."

"You think I care what you do?" he says, still scribbling. "People come and go. That's life. Best just to accept it. You can do what you want. I could care less."

"I don't believe you," I tell him.

"So?" He looks up at me with red around the edges of his eyes. "Why should I care about that, either?"

He looks away. His chair scrapes on the concrete as he pushes it back from the desk.

"Come on, let's go."

"Wait, there's a message." I point to the machine. "The light is blinking."

Tobin sits back down and pushes the big square button marked Play.

"Uh, this is a message for Lemonade . . . Lemonade, this is Eliza Rose. Um . . . yeah, so, we had this game of Capture the Flag at our house last night and everything and, um . . . we saw something out in our back woods. I'm wondering if you guys want to come out and investigate. You can call me back. . . ."

Tobin scribbles the phone number on the yellow legal pad.

He suddenly looks up at me. "Why would Eliza Rose ask for *you*?"

I stare at him, wide-eyed.

"I—ah, I don't, ah—"

He picks up the receiver and holds it toward me.

"Do you want to call her back?"

• • •

"I know, Mrs. Dickerson, but we never find *anything*," Tobin complains, holding his case in front of him on her front porch. "And we have another call to get to this morning."

"This time is different," Mrs. Dickerson tells us with a broad smile.

"Why's that?" Tobin asks.

"Because," she says, "this time I remembered the Polaroid."

I gasp, and Tobin drops his leather case on his foot.

"You didn't!" he exclaims.

"I did!" she says.

Her smile gets even bigger, and her eyes disappear in all her wrinkles. Then she pulls an instant photo out of her apron pocket and holds it out in front of us. Tobin grabs it and I scramble to get a look over his shoulder.

"Wow," I whisper, looking back at Mrs. Dickerson.

"It can't be," Tobin breathes.

"O ye of little faith," she sighs. "I told you one of these days I'd have the proof you're looking for. Now, who's hungry? I made M&M cookies and chocolate meringue clouds."

"We've got an eye!" Tobin calls out to Charlie when he pushes open the door at Bigfoot Souvenirs and More. "An actual *eye!*" He waves the picture in the air.

"What?" Charlie says from the front counter, where he's watching *The Phil Donahue Show* on a small black-and-white television set.

"Mrs. Dickerson got a picture!" Tobin runs over to him and holds the photo out. "And it's an eye, Charlie!"

"You're kidding!" Charlie exclaims.

"Look for yourself," I say. "It looks like an eye to me, too!"

Charlie takes the picture and examines it. Tobin pulls his magnifying glass out of his back pocket and hands it to Charlie.

"For goodness' sake," Charlie mutters, removing his glasses and examining the picture with the magnifying glass.

He passes it back to me.

It's not the greatest picture in the universe. Mrs. Dickerson said she shot it through the kitchen window, so there's a glare from the flash on the glass, and it's blurry in spots for sure. But there *is* one part that's clear as day.

An eye. An actual eye, with a pupil and a brown iris and reddish-brown skin and reddish-brown hair and a snippet of a wrinkled nose.

The rest is just blurry reddishness.

"We better call Professor Malcolm," I say.

"Bigfoot Detectives Inc. is going to go down in history!" Tobin shouts.

# 32

# OPERATION:
# ELIZA ROSE'S BACKYARD

"He was out there." Eliza Rose points toward the woods from her back porch later that morning.

My palms are sweating.

Not because of the Bigfoot, but because I'm praying that Eliza Rose doesn't say anything about the game of Kick the Can to Tobin. At least if I can tell him first, it won't be as bad as it would be hearing it from her.

"There?" Tobin follows the direction where her finger is pointing. "At the tree line?"

She nods.

Tobin and I start down the back porch steps. Eliza Rose hesitates on the top step, holding on to the pillar at the top of the stairs. I turn around and look at her.

"It scared me to death," she says.

There's fear in her eyes, and I really believe her. This isn't a hoax or a joke or a bear or a guy in a suit.

No one is laughing on the other end of the green phone now.

"It's okay," I tell her, reaching out to touch her arm. "Whatever it was is gone."

She smiles, looking a little embarrassed.

"Right, sorry. It was so scary. Can I just tell you the story from up here? I don't really want to go back out there."

"Sure," I say, ignoring the exasperated sigh leaking out of Tobin.

We all settle on the white wicker furniture with fluffy floral cushions, Eliza Rose on a rocking chair, me on the ottoman, and Tobin on a small bench against the porch rail.

"Tell us exactly what happened." Tobin has his pen poised over his yellow legal pad.

"Well, it was right when it was getting dark, and we were playing Capture the Flag that night," she starts, and then turns to me. "It's like Kick the Can, but not really. Joe Kelly was there, Mei Cunningham, Beau Stitch, and . . . oh, yeah, Nick French . . ." She starts listing names on her fingers. "And J-Man—doesn't he have the greatest dimples?"

I glance at Tobin.

His eyebrows are scrunched together, and he's looking at me suspiciously over his wire-rims.

"About the Bigfoot, Eliza Rose," I say.

"Right . . . yeah, so, me and Mei were on Nick French's team, and he had us hide our flag just inside the tree line under this dead tree on the ground. We found a hole in the tree and folded up the flag and hid it there. Technically, we weren't supposed to go into the forest, but Nick French goes, 'It's not like it's cheating,' and me and Mei said—"

"If we could get to the sighting sooner rather than later, that would be helpful," Tobin interrupts her.

I give him a look.

"What?" he asks.

She turns to me. "It's part of the story."

"Yeah, I get that," I say. "Take your time."

Tobin huffs another big sigh.

"Anyway, the other team tried and tried to find the flag, and couldn't, and it was getting dark, even though the back porch light was on. It was still dark, especially out there." She points to the woods. "My mom has been nagging at my dad to put more lights back here, but he's been so busy he just hasn't gotten to it, you know. . . ."

Tobin has stopped scribbling on his notepad and is holding his chin in his hand, staring at Eliza Rose with a completely annoyed look on his face.

"Anyway, the other team lost and got kind of mad, especially Joe Kelly and J-Man. You know, they're big babies anyway when it comes to losing. But they started accusing Nick of cheating by hiding the flag in the woods when we agreed that the tree line was the boundary. So we all headed to find the flag and—"

"And what?" Tobin bursts out with frustration, his arms wide in the air.

"That's when we saw it," she says.

"Saw what exactly, Eliza Rose?" I ask.

"That beast," she whispers.

"Ah . . . let me stop you there," Tobin says. "It's not a—"

"Let her finish." I hold my hand up, hoping to save us all from yet another Bigfoot Are People Too lecture.

"He was just standing there." She points to the woods again. "Crouched down behind the dead tree. Like he was . . ."

"Like he was what?" I ask.

"Watching us play," she says, and then laughs. "That sounds weird, doesn't it? But that's what it seemed like."

"What did you do?" I breathe.

"I don't know if I ever really thought it was true, you know?" she says. "I mean, I've heard the stories and all that, but there was this part of me that thought it was just a legend. A story that's not really true, you know?"

"Yes," I say.

"But it's not just a story." She turns to Tobin.

He's busy scribbling on his pad. When he's done, he looks up at her and leans forward on the bench.

"It's not a story, Eliza Rose," he says. "They're real."

"I know that now," she says.

"So, what did you do?" I ask again.

"I think I might have screamed . . . or at least someone did. Maybe it was Mei. It's hard to remember. Then everyone started yelling, and my daddy came running out of the house with a rifle, and—"

"A *rifle*?" Tobin stands straight up. "What the heck for?"

She looks at him in surprise.

"It's a wild animal loose in the woods. Would've been the same if it had been a bear or cougar or something that close to the yard. Actually, I think that's what he thought it was at first when he raced out of the house."

Tobin sighs and starts pacing the porch.

"What if he'd shot him?" he asks, pointing his pen at Eliza Rose.

She thinks about his question.

"Well, I guess then there'd finally be proof, and no one would ever doubt it again. You're lucky, Lem," she says to me. "If we'd seen that thing that day we all played Kick the Can, you'd be as scared as me."

Tobin turns to face me then.

I don't even know the words that would describe the look on his face. It's like a combination of surprise and hurt and anger and disgust, all at the same time.

He looks like I punched him hard in the gut and he never even saw it coming.

* * *

"A rifle!" Tobin exclaims while we trudge through Eliza Rose's backyard toward the tree line out back.

"You guys be careful!" Eliza Rose hollers after us from the safety of her wicker chair on the back porch.

"A rifle!" he says again. "Can you even imagine?"

"I know it, Tobin," I say. "I heard her. I was sitting right next to you."

"Why in the world would anyone want to kill a Bigfoot? It's the most idiotic thing I've ever heard of. See? What did I tell you about their modus operandi? Hiding. I'd do the same if I could. There's nothing worse than people. They're awful. I'd go and hide away forever with the Bigfoot if I could."

"What about your mom?"

"We'd let her visit," he says.

"And your dad?"

This time he ignores me.

When I see the fallen log at the tree line, I point to it.

"That must be it there," I say.

"I have eyes," he snaps. "You think I need you to point it out? I can do this all by myself. Why don't you just go back to HQ and man the phone in case we get another call?"

"See, I told you you were mad."

"How many times do I have to say I'm not mad? I don't care what you do."

"Good," I say. "Then you won't care if I stay."

Tobin sighs long and loud, setting his black leather case on top of the log, then trudges through the grass and pushes through low-hanging branches to look all around it.

"No footprints," he tells me. "Too grassy here."

I push through branches to the other side of the tree, scanning the woods. A mosquito lands on my arm, and I swat at it.

"What else should we look for?" I call to Tobin.

"Any signs that he was here." Tobin takes his magnifying glass out of his case. "Hair or scat."

Again with the number two. Disgusting.

We both push into the woods. Him in one direction, and me in the other. Even though it's sunny and warm, the light only sprinkles its glow between the tall pine branches reaching toward the sky. Birds are chirping and pinecones slowly fall between branches to the soft bed of needles below.

My stomach growls.

I wish I'd thought to bring a Twinkie with me. Especially since we didn't have time for even one of Mrs. Dickerson's meringue cloud cookies. Or time to order sandwiches from Diesel's.

Just when I'm about to give up, something grabs at the back of my head, pulling on my hair.

"Ouch!"

I reach behind me to try to free myself from a crooked branch, but the more I try, the more tangled I get. My fingers work at the knot, but while they do, hairs are being pulled straight out of my scalp. When I finally get myself undone, I can see that the branch has snagged a good handful of my curly red hair.

But that's not all I see.

Next to the long red hairs is an even bigger clump of thick reddish-brown fur.

"Tobin!" I scream. "I found something!"

# 33

# TERMINATION

Tobin is so excited about the hair sample that it seems like he's completely forgotten about the whole thing with Eliza Rose and the game of Kick the Can.

At first.

The very next day at the Bigfoot Headquarters, we call up Professor Malcolm all the way in Idaho to tell him what we found. Eliza Rose had given us a ziplock bag from the kitchen to collect the specimen. Tobin had pulled it off the tree branch with a pair of tweezers from his leather case.

"Less possibility of contamination," he told me.

Now he's holding the green receiver between our heads so I can listen in too.

"That's amazing, kids!" I can hear Professor Malcolm say. "Absolutely amazing!"

I want to say I'm the one who found it.

Me.

Lemonade Liberty Witt, Assistant Bigfoot Detective Extraordinaire.

But I don't.

I figure I'm already in the doghouse with Tobin, best just to let him take all the credit.

Which he does.

Thunder stealer.

"Did I tell you that I'm the president and founder of Bigfoot Detectives Inc.?" Tobin asks Professor Malcolm. "It is the mission of the corporation to be a leader in the scientific world of Bigfoot discovery." Then he turns to me and whispers, "Bigfoot Detectives Inc. is going down in history."

Professor Malcolm chuckles.

"You're right about making history!" he says. "Good job to both of you! If you can slip that sample in the mail to me, I can run tests on it to see if we can identify where it came from. And if you can get copies made of that image as well, I would love to have one. With your help, we might just add a new species to the list of primates!"

I don't think Tobin's chest could be bigger or his smile wider.

"We make a good team," I say after we hang up.

He doesn't say anything for a minute, and I watch the smile slip off his lips. Then he puts his hands on his hips and glares at me.

"You never answered me when I asked you how Eliza Rose knew you."

• • •

It's like watching an explosion in slow motion. Knowing it's coming and not being able to do anything about it. And the whole scene is even worse than I thought it'd be.

"You did *what*?" Tobin asks.

"I didn't think it was that big a deal," I say.

"No? Then why didn't you tell me about it, huh? Why didn't you tell me the truth that day when I asked you where you were? You said you were at Mrs. Dickerson's."

"I did go to Mrs. Dickerson's. She made finger sandwiches that didn't look like fingers at all. Egg salad fingers with no tomatoes. You can even ask her."

"And then to Nick French's."

"Well, so what, anyway?" I say. "It's a free country. I can have other friends."

"This isn't about having other friends, and you know it."

I do know it.

Deep down inside, I know it. And that's why I kept it a secret, I suppose. But what is deep inside and what is coming out of my mouth are not exactly in sync. My volcano is taking over, and the lava is flowing, and I can't seem to stop it.

And he can't seem to stop his, either.

"Just 'cause you don't have other friends, does that mean I can't?" I blow lava in his direction.

The look on his face is like I punched him in the gut again, then spit on his new shoes, and then stole his safari hat and threw it in the garbage.

It's too far.

And I know it as soon as it comes out of my mouth. If I was a cartoon character, I would have been trying to grab the words back before they reached him, letter by letter.

I picture my cartoon character trying to take back the words. But life isn't as easy as *The Bugs Bunny Show*. It's real. Tobin hears the words I spew at him loud and clear. I know it because the whites of his eyes turn redder.

"They're mean to me." His voice sounds high and squeaky.

I sigh and drop my head.

"I know it, Tobin. Maybe if you came with me, they'd see you differently. Like how I see you."

"What in the world makes you think I would want to be friends with any of them?"

"I think you do," I tell him.

"Wrong!" he tells me.

"I think I'm right."

"Wrong again!"

"Look at how good friends we are. Maybe they could even help us, you know, be a part of the Inc. in some way."

"Never!" Tobin's voice is loud now. "I don't need them! I don't need *anyone*! Not even you! I'm sorry I ever even met you!"

"Well, maybe I feel the same about you!" I shout back at him.

"I don't want you working here anymore," he says, looking me straight in the eye.

"You can't be serious."

"I am serious. Turn in your name badge and see yourself out. You are officially relieved of your position as assistant Bigfoot detective with Bigfoot Detectives Inc."

"Tobin—"

He holds out his hand palm up, waiting for his stupid handmade badge with the Elmer's glue clumped up on the back.

I stare at him, and he stares at me.

"Fine," I say, pulling it off my T-shirt.

I throw it on top of the desk.

"Leave." He points to the door.

I don't know what else to say. I stomp toward the door and put my hand on the rusty knob. Before I open it, I turn around to look at him one more time.

He's already got his head buried in his ridiculous yellow legal pad, and he's shuffling the papers furiously.

"Are you sure you want to do this?" I ask him.

"Already done," he says.

"Fine, have it your way," I say, pulling the door open.

The whole garage door rattles when I give the side door one good hard slam. And then I walk away without even once looking back.

# 34

# HOLD THE PICKLES

Charlie and I eat dinner alone. He's ordered deli sandwiches from Diesel's.

Again.

Egg salad. With tomatoes.

Again.

The fact that he still hasn't cared enough to figure out that I hate tomatoes makes me want to scream. Miss Cotton would know on the first day I lived with her. And if not the first, then for sure the second.

"Where's Tobin tonight?" Charlie asks, taking a bite of his BLT on rye. "I got him his usual, ham and cheese, hold the pickles."

I roll my eyes at the pickle comment as I'm forced to pull each slimy tomato off with my fingers and put them on the side of my plate.

"How should I know?" I ask. "I'm not his keeper. Am I supposed to be in charge of him or something? Because I'm not."

Charlie stops chewing and looks at me with a perplexed expression.

"And just so you know, I hate tomatoes. I don't know why you haven't figured that out yet," I tell him. "I only have to pick them out with my fingers *every time.*"

He starts chewing again, then swallows, and then takes a long drink of his iced tea.

"Did you and Tobin have a fight?" he finally asks.

"He had a fight. I didn't have a fight. You said there was nothing wrong with playing with the others, and you were wrong. He thought there was plenty wrong with it."

"Did you call Professor Malcolm today?"

"Yeah."

"What did he say?"

"He wants us to send him the hair sample, and he'll test it and bring us back the results."

"That's wonderful news! Aren't you excited? Tobin must be ecstatic. You don't know where he is?"

"I said I didn't," I say again, louder this time. "I mean, am I supposed to babysit that kid or something? Are we expected to be joined at the hip?"

"Lemonade." Charlie sets down his sandwich and leans in close across the table. "Why are you shouting at me?"

"He fired me!" I push my plate away.

Charlie looks confused.

"That doesn't sound like Tobin."

"Well, it's exactly what he did!"

"What happened?"

"You said he'd understand about going to Nick French's. You said it wasn't a big deal."

"Didn't take it well, I gather?"

"No. He took my badge away, and he fired me. Me! I found the footprints and the hair sample, and he fired *me*!"

Charlie leans back in his chair.

"He's a very sensitive kid," he says. "He carries a lot of pain inside him. I think if anyone could understand that, it would be you."

"Take his side, why don't you!"

"I—I'm not taking anyone's side, Lem, I'm just saying—"

"I wish I'd never come to this place!" I shout from deep inside my volcano. "I wish I'd never even heard of Willow Creek, or that stupid beast of yours that lives out in these woods."

Charlie takes a deep breath and pushes his chair back.

"You came here for a reason, Lem."

"Only because Mama died. That's it. She didn't want anything to do with this place when she was alive, either!"

I feel like I'm being sucked deep in the quicksand and he doesn't even notice.

Just like he hasn't figured it out about the stupid tomatoes.

There's no big, strong hand to reach for me now. I'm sinking fast. He's too busy searching for Tobin.

Saving Tobin.

Ordering *hold the pickles* for Tobin.

My volcano is out of control, spewing hot lava every-where I go. And I can't stop it.

"I hate it here! And so did Mama!"

I get up from the table and start to run.

I want to run until I make it all the way home. Then I can forget this place and all the people in it. The screen door slams behind me. It's already dark. Low thunder rolls. But I don't even care if it storms all over me. I keep running and running and running.

Running until I can't hear Charlie calling my name any-more.

* * *

The rain comes somewhere between Nick French's house and Mrs. Dickerson's place. It comes at first in small, bitty sprinkles, and then in sloppy splashes that hit the top of my head and leak into my eyes. Soon the splashes turn to buckets.

But I keep running.

Cracks of thunder and flashes of light wage a war above me. But tonight I'm not even scared, because tonight I'm hoping that one of those strikes of lightning finds its way to earth and zaps me into dust. Then I won't ever have to think of anything again.

Not Mama.

Not Tobin.

Not Charlie.

Not Delores Jaworski.

Not even whatever is hiding in the woods.

Then maybe I'll be free from the quicksand waiting to suck me in and never let me breathe again. Free of the load that is just too heavy for me to carry.

I keep running until I find myself knocking on Mrs. Dickerson's screen door, drenched to the bone.

Some rain. But mostly tears.

"Lemonade Liberty Witt!" Mrs. Dickerson exclaims, pushing the door open. She is lipstick-less and her long white hair blows free in the wind. "Sweet girl, you come inside this instant. What in the world are you doing out on a night like this?"

"I don't—I don't—we had a fight . . . and I—"

"Okay . . . well, never you mind. You're here now, let's get you into something warm and dry."

She takes me into the front bedroom and digs through a stash of clothes in a dresser drawer near the bed.

"Let's see here," she says, rummaging through folded piles while I drip on the hardwood floor and shiver. "I always have something on hand for the grandchildren when they come to visit. Yes, here we go. This should do nicely . . . and . . . let's see, ah, this too, maybe. Here, sweetheart, put these on and put your wet clothes in the tub."

"Thank you," I say through chattering teeth.

"Hurry up now, before you catch pneumonia."

After I towel off and get changed in the bathroom, I find Mrs. Dickerson in the kitchen heating up water for tea and pulling cookies out of the cookie jar. I hope she has some meringue clouds left from the other day. I didn't even get to try them.

"Now, have a seat and we can talk." She points to the

kitchen table, already set with cloth napkins and teacups on saucers. In the center of the table are a tiny pitcher of milk, a jar of honey, and a bowl full of lemon wedges.

I pull a chair out and sit down. I'm still shivering. The teakettle whistles on the stove, and she pours steaming water into my cup and then into hers. The rain clicks on the kitchen window. I wrap my frozen fingers around the warm cup and put my face over the steam to heat my nose and cheeks. I watch the tea from the bag seep into the water in slow waves until the water is all brown, while Mrs. Dickerson settles in a seat across from me.

"I already tried to phone Charlie, but he didn't answer. He must be worried sick."

I don't say anything.

"Now, please tell me what happened," she says.

The tears come fast, even though I thought I couldn't possibly have one more left. I tell her all about Tobin firing me, and Charlie and the tomatoes, and Tobin's pickle-less sandwich, and how Delores Jaworski came to the store, and Kick the Can, and Rainbow, and everything else. I tell her that everyone here in Willow Creek hates me. My words spill over each other because they can't get out fast enough.

"I wish I'd never even come here," I finally say. "It's been a complete and total disaster."

She takes a long, deep breath and then a slow sip of tea with her eyes closed.

"My goodness, that *is* a bad day, isn't it?" she says to me after setting her cup on its saucer.

I nod. "The worst day in the world. Well . . . not the worst, but it's up there."

She nods.

"That last day with Mama—" I start, but can't finish.

She reaches across the table and touches my hand.

"Lemonade, do you remember when I spoke to you about your mother and Charlie?" she asks.

"Yes."

"Remember when I told you that sometimes when people are grieving badly, those sad feelings can come out in the wrong way?"

"Yes, I remember."

"You have all lost someone or something important, haven't you? You're all grieving that loss in your own ways."

"Yes," I say. "I guess so."

"You've lost your dear, lovely mother. A beautiful person inside and out."

I swallow the lump.

"Tobin has lost his brave and dutiful father. A good man who loved his family with everything he had inside him."

"Yes," I whisper.

"And Charlie has lost twice. First his wonderful wife, and then his lovely daughter. How devastated he would be to lose what's most important to him now."

"Tobin?" I ask.

"You, sweet Lemonade. You."

"He doesn't care about me," I tell her, staring at my china cup. "Not as much as he cares about Tobin. I told you about the pickles, didn't I? *Didn't* I? He doesn't want me here, anyhow. He never did. He could care less if I up and move back to San Francisco."

She looks at me curiously. "What makes you say that?"

I think hard about her question.

I think of the books Charlie has brought home for me, the comforter, the steamy milk, the space in the hall where I swiped the picture of Mama. I think of Rainbow, and his great big hand reaching out for me.

I shrug.

"I just know it," I say. "And Tobin hates me too. He took my badge and everything."

"I know Charlie loves you more than anything. And he would give anything to have another chance to make things right with Elizabeth. Sad feelings can take control of us and make us choose things we wouldn't normally choose."

"Like mean words," I say.

"Exactly, sweetheart."

"I said mean things to both Charlie and Tobin. I didn't know how to stop them. They just kept coming up and flying out, and I couldn't take them back."

"They love you." She smiles at me. "I'm sure they're hurting just as you are. I bet they would love to change today just as much as you would."

"I don't know," I say.

"You really don't want to leave Willow Creek, do you?"

The lump gets bigger and bigger, and my eyes blur with tears, until I burst.

"No!" I cry out, wiping my eyes with the back of my hand. "I want to stay here with Charlie and with you and with Tobin and Debbie and with Mr. Harold and all the kids I've met—"

Mrs. Dickerson comes over to my side of the table and hugs me hard.

The phone rings.

"I'll bet that's Charlie now, out of his mind with worry." She straightens and moves her cane toward the yellow phone on the wall.

"Hello? Yes, I—"

She turns her back to me.

"Oh, no," she whispers. "Oh, my God . . . Yes, we'll be right there."

She slips the receiver back on the wall and turns to look at me.

"What's wrong?" I ask.

"Oh, honey. There's been an accident."

# 35

# GRANDFATHER

Mrs. Dickerson drives an old red Volkswagen Beetle with rust on the back fender. It makes a buzzing noise when the speedometer gets over fifty-five miles per hour.

It buzzes the whole way to the hospital.

But that's the only thing I really remember about getting there, because my brain is too busy worrying. When we finally make it, Debbie is waiting for us in her white nurse's uniform, white shoes, and a white nurse's hat. Tobin is sitting on a stuffed bench welded to the wall, twisting his fingers in knots and then untwisting them again.

"Where is he?" I demand, running toward Debbie down a long hall. "Where's Charlie?"

She bends at the waist to face me eye to eye, her arms wide to catch me. When I reach them, they feel like a life vest keeping me from going under, and I feel my legs let me go.

"Shh," she says gently, holding me tight. "It's going to be okay."

"No!" I cry. "No, it isn't! He's hurt because of me! Because of *me*! It won't ever be okay again. Not ever!"

I feel a hand on my shoulder and turn to see Tobin by my side now. Tobin in his khaki shorts, red T-shirt, and that stupid safari hat strapped tight under his chin, peering over his glasses at me.

He grabs my hand without saying a word.

I hold it tight.

Mrs. Dickerson is still scooting her cane down the hall to catch up to us, and when she does, she places her arm around me too.

And then we all hug.

One giant hug. It feels warm and safe and comfortable and familiar. It feels like a family. Maybe not by blood, but by choice.

And by love.

A feeling I thought would never, ever exist again in my whole life. The lump is back, and I don't even try to swallow it down.

I just let myself cry.

• • •

Even though Charlie is still sleeping, and it's way past visiting hours, and kids aren't really supposed to be in the rooms because they have too many germs on their hands, Debbie gives me permission to see him. But only after I scrub my hands twice with disinfectant soap and swear I'll stay no more than five minutes.

"He's going to be okay," she says. "But he needs to rest right now, so you can only stay a few minutes."

"I promise," I tell her, crossing an X over my chest.

Tobin and Mrs. Dickerson watch from the bench while Debbie pushes open the thick wooden door of Charlie's room.

Charlie.

*Charlie Milford Witt* is printed in bold letters on a metal chart hanging from the end of his bed.

*Charlie Milford Witt.*

He is still. His eyes closed. Lying in bed with the covers pulled up under his arms and tucked tight around him, the two-thirds of what's left of his hair in a mess.

He's pale. Even paler than Eliza Rose was on that afternoon she told us about her Bigfoot sighting.

I stand next to the bed staring at him. Looking at him in a hospital bed reminds me of the last time I saw Mama.

Sick and weak and pale.

Machines and cords and tubes intertwined.

The beeping of the heart and breathing machines.

"Lemonade," she whispered that last day. "You are the love of my life, sweet girl. I wish I could stay here with you, but I can't. Always remember that we are connected, no matter what. I am a part of you as you are a part of me. I will always be in your heart. I will be a part of your spirit. You are my Lemonade. You are strong and smart and will always find a way to make sweet whatever bad comes your way."

I crawled up in bed with her and laid my head on her shoulder, watching her chest slowly rise up and then sink down.

Up and then down.

Up and then down.

Until it didn't move up and then down anymore.

A doctor put his hand on my back and told me it was time to say good-bye.

"Mama," I whisper to her now. "Look what I did, Mama. Look what I did. And now I don't know what to do. I can't make it sweet. I don't know how. Help me, Mama. I need you."

I wipe tears with my palms.

"Please, Mama, tell me what to do. I've made a mess of things, and I don't know how to fix it. I don't. I can't make lemonade anymore. . . . I forgot how."

The room is quiet except for the beeping of the machines around me. Just like that last day with her. My guts feel all twisted up inside my stomach.

I crawl up on the bed next to Charlie and lay my head on his shoulder, watching his chest move up and then down.

Up and then down.

Up and then down.

Machines beep and air rushes through tubes resting inside his nose.

More tears find their way down my cheeks and onto his chest. So many that I'm drowning.

I can't breathe.

I can't stop.

I'm slipping into sadness quicksand, and not even Charlie will find me. I'll slip away, and no one will ever be able to save me.

"Please, Mama," I whisper again into his chest. "I need you, Mama, and you're not here. Please, Mama, please tell God not to take my grandfather, too."

# 36

# TIME TO SQUEEZE THE LEMONS

I wake up the next morning underneath my fluffy comforter.

Rainbow in my arms.

Dishes clink in the kitchen like any other morning, and I can smell coffee brewing.

Charlie.

Getting the sticks and seeds and bark ready.

Having his usual coffee.

Black. No sugar.

Maybe it was all just a bad dream. A horrible nightmare.

When I push the covers off me, I see I'm still wearing Mrs. Dickerson's Willow Creek sweatshirt and shorts from the bottom drawer of the dresser in her spare room.

And I know it's no dream.

I drag myself out of bed, my arms, legs, and whole body tired from the heavy load.

The floorboards squeak underneath me as I tiptoe down the hall and peek around the corner to the kitchen.

"About time," Tobin says to me, stuffing a piece of bacon in his mouth and snapping in another blue puzzle piece. "Look, Lemonade. We only have one yarn ball left."

Debbie turns around from the stove.

"Good morning, Lemonade." She smiles. "I'm making breakfast sandwiches with eggs and bacon. Grab a plate, honey."

"I'm not hungry," I tell her, pulling a chair out next to Tobin.

He's staring at me like I'm some kind of alien who just crash-landed out in the yard and then came in for breakfast.

"What are you looking at?" I ask him.

"What do you think I'm looking at?" he says.

"I mean, why are you staring at me like that?"

"Then why didn't you say that in the first place?"

"Tobin!" I say, exasperated.

"I don't know," he says. "I guess because I want to know how you are and I don't know how to ask you, so I'm just watching you to see if I can tell on my own. But I can't tell on my own, so I guess I'll just have to ask you anyhow."

"That depends on how Charlie is," I say, turning to Debbie.

She comes over to the table holding an open-faced breakfast sandwich with sunny-side-up eggs that are runny in the middle and two burnt-on-the-edges strips of bacon on top. She's wearing her faded Levi's with holes in the knees, a yellow T-shirt, and a matching bandana in her hair. She has blush on her cheeks and small silver hoops in her ears.

"I got a call from the hospital this morning, honey." She places a warm hand on my head. "Charlie is awake and doing well. He's going to be just fine, Lem."

"You promise?"

"Promise."

I lay my head on my arms on the table and cry. I probably have yolk stuck in my hair and bacon grease too, but I don't even care.

I just cry and cry and cry.

Debbie is sitting next to me, her head on my shoulder. "Sweet girl," she says softly. "I know how hard things have been for you. It'll get better, I promise you it will."

"I—I don't know how," I sputter through the tears.

"What do you mean, honey?"

"How to make it better," I tell her, lifting my head up to face her.

I feel Tobin's hand on my other shoulder then, and I turn to face him, wiping my nose with my forearm.

"By making lemonade, that's how." He pats my shoulder like you pat a German shepherd. "You said you know how to make it, isn't that right?"

"I used to know," I tell him. "But I think I forgot."

"Well, it's probably still in there somewhere," he says matter-of-factly, and then goes back to his yarn ball.

I turn to Debbie.

"He makes a lot of sense sometimes." She smiles at me.

I look at him.

He's examining a blue puzzle piece over his wire-rims. Then he finds just the right spot for it and snaps it into place. He looks up at us and smiles.

"What?" he asks.

I turn to Debbie.

"Yeah," I say. "Yeah, he does."

# 37

# DEEP-DOWN LOVE

After breakfast, Debbie helps me get ready so we can all go back to the hospital to visit Charlie. I watch her in the bathroom mirror while she gently brushes the knots out of my curls. She's helping me tie a bandana in my hair just like hers. She found me a pink one back at her place and then we picked out a pink top from my chest of drawers to go with it.

I study her while she concentrates on detangling the red jungle. She looks a lot like Tobin. Mostly in the eyes and the lips.

"You miss him, don't you?" I finally ask her.

"Who? Charlie?"

"No . . . Scotty."

She stops brushing then and her eyes meet mine in the mirror.

They're exactly the same color as Tobin's. Bright blue with tiny specks of brown inside.

"Yes," she says softly, starting to brush the knots again. "Very much. I'm sure just as much as you miss your mom."

I sigh and lean on the counter in front of me, my chin in my hand.

"I miss her so much sometimes my insides hurt. Like worse than having the flu."

"I know that ache," she says. "I know it very well."

"What do you do when you hurt so bad inside that you don't know what to do with yourself?"

She takes a long time to think about her answer. I can tell she's thinking because she looks just like Tobin when she's doing it. Serious and intense.

"I guess I try to think about some of the best times I can remember with him. And sometimes it turns that ache into happiness. Happiness that I had Scotty in my life at all. Even if I don't get to keep him forever here on earth, I get to keep him forever in here." She points to her heart.

"I know exactly what you mean. I have so many good memories of the times I spent with Mama, I can't even count them all."

She meets my eyes again and grins real big at me in the mirror. Then she stops brushing and pulls herself up on the counter next to me. "Tell me one. A wonderful memory of your mom. I'd love to hear it."

"You would?"

"Of course I would."

Now it's my turn to think really hard.

"There are so many," I tell her. "It's hard to choose."

She nods like she understands. And I know she really does.

"Every Saturday morning I'd get up early and crawl into bed with her and we'd cuddle together. And then we'd get up and walk to Piper's Bakery near the pier and get hot tea and the biggest, stickiest, gooiest bear claws you've ever seen. Then we'd go down by the water to find a bench and we'd eat the bear claws and we'd catch up on what happened during the week. I'd tell her all about my friends at school and she'd tell me all about the animals that came to see her and their owners, too."

"That sounds wonderful," Debbie says.

"Saturdays were my most favorite day of the week because of that."

She smiles. "I can see why."

"Now you tell me one," I say, putting my hand on her knee.

"Okay," she says, covering my hand with hers. "When I was pregnant with Tobin, I had to spend some time in bed and I was so bored and tired of being in bed all the time. And Scotty came home from work every day with a single tulip to put in the vase next to my bed. Just because I couldn't get outside to enjoy them. And then he would go down to the kitchen and make us open-faced breakfast sandwiches for dinner with sunny-side-up eggs and crispy bacon on top. Because that's what I was craving back then. Then we'd sit in bed together and watch Johnny Carson while we shared a bowl of Neapolitan ice cream. I ate all the strawberry and he always complained I didn't share it with him." She laughs to herself. "I stuck him with the vanilla and chocolate every time."

I laugh too. "Is that why you only buy strawberry ice cream?" I ask her.

Her eyes get wide. "Yes," she says. "How did you—"

"Tobin said you only buy strawberry even though vanilla goes best with chocolate cake."

"Oh, yes, he tells me that again and again." She smiles to herself. "I guess I buy it for Scotty . . . for when . . . if . . . he comes home."

"You love him a whole lot, don't you?"

"Deeply. Just like you love your mother."

"Deep-down love," I say.

"Yes," she says. "Deep-down love."

"Charlie said Scotty wrote you a letter."

"Yes," she says quietly. "I keep it with me all the time. I guess it makes me feel closer to him. To read his words. How much he loved us."

"I know what you mean," I tell her. "I keep Rainbow right on top of my bed now. Even though she doesn't smell like Mama anymore. I know that once she held that rabbit close to her and when I hold it close to me it's almost like . . . like she's holding *me* again. The way she used to."

She smiles. "I remember Rainbow."

"You do?"

"Oh, yes."

I smile too now and know that Debbie's right. Thinking of memories with Mama does make the ache inside me feel better. Because it's like for that moment she's here with me again.

Debbie looks at me. "Thank you for sharing your memory with me. And thank you for letting me share mine."

Then she jumps down from the counter and wraps her arms around me.

"You're very special, Lemonade Liberty Witt. I'm so glad I get to know you."

Her arms feel nice around me. Kind of like it felt when Mama's were around me, but different, too.

Nice different.

• • •

At ten-fifteen hours (really 10:15 a.m.), we all pile into Debbie's copper-colored Pinto and head back to the hospital to visit Charlie. Tobin lets me ride shotgun without my even having to call it first.

On the way there my palms are wet and my stomach is still queasy.

I bite my fingernails the whole way across Highway 299, then all down Davis, and even down Blue Lake Boulevard, where the hospital is. By the time we get there, my thumb is bleeding a little, and it aches because I bit it too far down.

Charlie's room is number 11. When we get to his door, I push it open.

"Well, there they all are!" Charlie says with a big smile on his face.

He's sitting up in bed with a book. I scramble up on the bed next to him and wrap my arms around his neck. He looks more surprised than I've ever seen him, but he wraps his arms around me and gives me a big, warm hug back.

"I'm so sorry, Charlie!" I burst out, my cheek on his shoulder. "I'm just so sorry!"

"Oh, Lem, it's not your fault," he tells me, squeezing me tight. "I'm the one who slipped on the rocks. That was all me."

"But if it wasn't for me, you wouldn't have been out there to begin with." I pull away to face him. "Out in the rain, looking for me."

"Well, I suppose that's true," he tells me. "But wherever you go, I'm going to follow you . . . you know why?"

"Why?"

"Because . . ." He clears his throat. "Because I love you, that's why."

Did he just say *love*?

Love?

Me?

Lemonade Liberty Witt?

After everything that's happened?

After I spewed lava in every direction?

Even though I forgot how to make lemonade?

I look up at him, and he gives me another big squeeze. And it feels like I'm being pulled from the quicksand. His face tells me that he's been there the whole time, making sure I didn't sink too deep, waiting for me to figure a way out on my own. But when I slipped farther . . . he gave me his hand.

That big, strong hand with a special silver band.

Just like the night we made warm milk on the stove.

"Okay, okay, enough of this." He clears his throat a bunch of times. "I have a very important question for you all. There's nothing but salt-free chicken, runny mashed potatoes, and watery Jell-O in this place. Did someone bring me a bag of Tibetan yak jerky?"

Everyone laughs.

Even me.

# 38

# IN TRIPLICATE

"I am officially reinstating you as a Bigfoot Detectives Inc. employee," Tobin tells me that evening after the hospital.

He pulls my Assistant Bigfoot Detective tag with the wad of Elmer's out of the drawer of the desk at the Bigfoot Headquarters and pins it to my front. He stands back, cocks his head to the side, and puckers up his lips, checking to see if it's straight.

### LEMONADE LIBERTY WITT
#### Assistant Bigfoot Detective

I touch the edges of the badge like it's gold. I can't believe I'm admitting this, but I've actually missed the stupid thing pinned to my front. It makes me feel important and part of something big.

"Raise your right hand," he says, holding his hand high in the air.

"Oh, come on! Is that really necessary?"

"Of course it's necessary."

I give him my biggest eye roll ever.

"*I, Lemonade Liberty Witt, promise not to blab any top secret, Bigfoot-related matters . . .*"

I repeat it.

"*To any source, including all newspapers and TV reporters, corporate spies, and any and all naysayers, while employed at Bigfoot Detectives Inc., for eternity or longer.*"

I repeat that, too.

"*And I will follow the lead of the Bigfoot Detectives Inc. founder and president and stop asking so many questions . . .*"

"Come on!" I drop my hand.

He smiles. "Okay, that's good enough, I guess. I'll type up the reinstatement paperwork tonight. I'll need it signed and sent back in triplicate."

"In what?"

"In triplicate," he says. "You know, one copy for you, one for me, and one for the file."

"Why do you have to make everything so hard?"

"What's hard about triplicate?"

"Well, first off, it's a waste of time."

"Yeah, but it's the rules."

"Your rules."

"So? Without rules things would run amuck and then life would just be anarchy . . . a ruleless, leaderless society. Then the next thing you know, you'll want to move the message pad . . . anarchy. You want that?"

"A little anarchy never hurt anyone," I tell him.

"Actually, anarchy has been the downfall of many societies. During the Neolithic Period—"

"Okay, okay." I hold out my hands, sensing one of his twenty-minute lists coming my way. "You win. I'll sign it in triplicate."

He smiles again.

He likes it when he wins.

Or maybe he's just happy because everything is back to the way it was. The way it should be.

I smile then too.

● ● ●

A week after Charlie gets out of the hospital, everything is back to normal.

Mostly.

Charlie's almost all better, except for the stitches sewn into his right eyebrow and the bandage taped over it to keep the germs out. Professor Malcolm is on his way from Idaho to give us the results from the test of the hair sample we sent him. He called Charlie last night to tell us that the local news wants to interview Tobin and me about our findings.

That morning, I choose my yellow sundress with the tiny daisies, the one that Mama bought me for a trip to the San Francisco Playhouse for her birthday last year. I carefully comb my hair and let my red curls hang loose down my back.

"Well, look at you," Charlie says when I come to the kitchen table. "Don't you look like a shiny new penny?"

"Thanks, Charlie, it's—" I stop and stare at Tobin.

He is sitting at the kitchen table in a crisp striped short-sleeved shirt with a clip-on polka-dot bow tie and long khaki pants with shiny brown dress shoes. His reddish-brown curls are parted on the side and slicked down into one big wave over his eyebrows.

Minus one tan safari hat strapped tight under his chin.

"What happened to you?" I ask, giggling behind my hand. Tobin sighs.

"My mother." He scowls. "My mother happened to me."

Charlie and I look at each other and laugh.

"Well, I think you look nice," I say, pulling out a chair.

"She took my hat." He pouts, shoveling in his seedy cereal.

"Yeah," I say. "I noticed that first thing."

• • •

Charlie closes the store for the afternoon to make sure there aren't any interruptions when the news people are filming. Even though the crew isn't scheduled until three o'clock, Professor Malcolm makes it to the store around one-thirty. When Tobin sees he's wearing a crisp shirt and sports jacket, he finally wipes the scowl off his face.

After we all say our hellos, we sit on the fluffy pillows around the fireplace.

"Kids," Professor Malcolm says, "I wanted to let you know the results of the testing in person, before the reporters get here."

Tobin looks like he's going to bust wide open and explode Tobin guts all over Bigfoot Souvenirs and More. I want to remind him to breathe, but I figure it will come to him on his own at some point.

"Yes, Professor Malcolm." I swallow.

"First of all, the footprint you casted is extraordinary. It measures fifteen and three quarters inches, and there is a distinct midtarsal break. It's undeniable."

Tobin and I look at each other again. And now I have to remind myself to breathe.

"And second, the fur sample you collected isn't bear fur," he says. "It isn't elk or moose or anything hoofed."

He pauses.

"What is it, then?" I finally exclaim.

"I can't identify it."

Another pause.

"What does that mean, Professor Malcolm?" Charlie asks.

"It means it doesn't match any *known* hair sample of common wildlife from the region . . . or elsewhere, for that matter. It has some resemblances to human hair, but it has never been cut. What I can say with certainty is that it is an unknown primate species."

"Primate?" Charlie asks.

"That's right." Professor Malcolm smiles. "It's not fur. It's primate hair."

Tobin looks at me.

"We did it, Lemonade!" Tobin jumps up and starts hugging me. "We did it!"

• • •

"You see, their modus operandi is to hide," Tobin is telling Channel Four News.

"Tell us more about that, Tobin," the woman reporter says, holding a microphone close to him. She's dressed fancy like the women in San Francisco, with high heels and a silk blue dress, and her hair is pulled back from her face by shiny barrettes on either side of her head.

"You see, they *need* to hide in this world," Tobin says, leaning his mouth real close to the microphone. "Because they're different. And people choose not to understand those that are different. And can become . . . cruel."

"I see," the woman says, and then looks at me. "Why is it that you've become a part of this?" she asks, holding the microphone out to me.

The man carrying the camera on his shoulder turns the large round lens in my direction, and I start to feel hot.

"I–I . . . ah," I start. "We, um, we just want to prove the species exists." I look at Tobin out of the corner of my eye, and he nods. "And, um, and to allow them to be protected so, ah, that they can live safely, just as any other creature on earth should . . . even if they are different." Tobin nods again. "Because sometimes it's the differences that are exactly what make us special."

I turn to Tobin and he turns to me and then he grins real big. And so does the news lady.

"Wonderfully put, Lemonade Liberty Witt," she says.

The camera guy makes a circular gesture with his hand, and the lady nods to him.

"Thank you very much, Tobin, Lemonade, Charlie, and Professor Malcolm, for your time today. This is Jessica Samish with Channel Four News and Bigfoot Detectives Inc. in Willow Creek, California. Back to you in the Redding studio, Tom."

# 39

# NEVER LETTING GO

That Sunday, Charlie decides to knock number three off my list of things he didn't used to know about me. The most embarrassing one.

3. I never learned to ride a bike.

"There you go, Lemonade! You got it! You got it!"

That's Charlie hollering behind me while I'm pedaling down the street in front of the house. He has his hand on the silver bar on the back of my green-and-pink-striped banana seat.

He promised me he wouldn't let me go.

And I believe him now more than ever.

I also know for sure, because I can hear him breathing real hard behind me as he tries to keep up with my pedaling.

Tobin and Debbie are sitting in the cheering section located on the yellow porch swing.

"Look at you go, Lemonade!" Debbie cheers.

"You're leaning too much to the right!" Tobin hollers.

I pedal until I reach the stop sign, and turn the silver handlebars to the left, make a shaky U-turn, and begin pedaling back toward the cheering crowd. Lucky for me, Charlie is still there to keep me vertical.

"Can I let go now?" Charlie asks, huffing and puffing.

"Only if you want Lemonade splatter all over the pavement!" I holler back at him.

"You can do this on your own. I know you can!" he shouts.

I take a deep breath.

"You promise?" I ask.

"I promise!"

"Okay, now!" I throw over my shoulder. "Do it now!"

I don't feel him let go, even though I know he does. At first I wiggle a little, trying to find a new balance without him.

And then I'm pedaling.

And I'm steering.

And I'm doing it all by myself.

Me!

I can hear Charlie yelling from behind me.

"I told you! I told you! Look at you go!"

I make it all the way back up the street and turn into the driveway, stopping next to Jake and moving the kickstand out with my tennis shoe. Charlie is jogging to catch up.

"You did it! Didn't I tell you?" He smiles big. "Not a scratch on you, and no Lemonade splatter on the pavement either!"

"I can ride a bike," I tell him, holding my arms up in victory.

He wraps his big arms around me, picks me up, and bearhugs me. I bury my face in his checkered shirt. He smells like Irish Spring soap and coffee beans and Old Spice cologne.

I know it's a smell I'll never forget, just like Mama and her strawberry Suave.

"Thanks, Charlie . . . I mean . . . Grandfather," I whisper into his shoulder.

He doesn't say anything. But I know he hears it, because he squeezes me even tighter.

• • •

That night in celebration of my great accomplishment, Charlie takes me, Tobin, and Debbie to dinner at the Arthur Treacher's Fish & Chips all the way in Redding. We toast my achievement with root beer floats for dessert. Debbie probably would have ordered strawberry ice cream for her float if they had it, but they don't.

When we all have our floats, Charlie pushes his chair out and stands up.

"To Lemonade." Charlie holds his Arthur Treacher's cup high in the air.

Tobin, Debbie, and I all raise our cups high in the air too.

"To Lemonade!" Debbie cheers.

"To Lemonade," Tobin repeats.

"And to those who should be here with us celebrating on this fine evening," Charlie goes on. "To Elizabeth, Rebecca, and Scotty. Wherever you may be, we know you are all here with us tonight and in our hearts forever."

"Hear, hear!" Debbie exclaims.

"Where?" Tobin asks, looking around.

"No, Tobin. It just means I agree," Debbie explains.

"Oh. Here, here, then." He shrugs.

I laugh.

"Let's all share one thing we miss about them." I look at Debbie and then at Charlie.

They both nod in agreement, and Charlie sits back down.

I point to Tobin. "You start."

He's in the middle of taking a big gulp of his float, and when he comes up for air, he has a foamy mustache.

"I miss my dad reading to me before bed. He always read me something about cryptozoology. He knew everything about it. Even more than me, if you can believe it." He takes another big gulp.

"Debbie," I say. "Your turn."

"Okay, um, I miss his kindness. He always practiced the Golden Rule. Do unto others as you would have them do unto you."

"Charlie?" I point in his direction.

"Oh, boy, let's see . . . I miss everything about your grandmother. One thing, uh . . . well, I guess I could pick her gardening. She used to have the most beautiful garden in town."

"Yes, she did." Debbie smiles.

"It was filled with flowers. Every color you can imagine. There wasn't a day that went by when she didn't have a vase of flowers on our kitchen table. Except for the winter, of course."

I think about Mama and her daisies on our kitchen counter, and I wish I could have met my grandmother.

I bet Mama was the spitting image of her.

"Okay, Lemonade. Your turn," Charlie says to me.

I think real hard about which thing to share about Mama.

"I know she is here right now and I know she's happy we have each other to share our memories."

"Here, here!" Tobin hollers, raising his float again.

"Hear, hear!" we all say.

# 40

# SCHOOLING TOBIN

There are exactly fourteen days left of summer. Tobin and I are at the Bigfoot Headquarters on Sunday. Tobin is shuffling through his yellow legal pad, and I'm reading another book that Charlie brought home for me. This one is called *Philip Hall Likes Me. I Reckon Maybe.* I've read it twice already.

The green phone rings, making us both jump.

Tobin nods at me. I grab the carefully written index card that's lined up next to the message pad and pick up the receiver.

"*Good afternoon . . . ,*" I read. "*And thank you for calling Bigfoot Detectives Inc., serving Willow Creek since 1974. This is Lemonade Liberty Witt, Assistant Bigfoot Detective. How may we help you with your Bigfoot needs today?*"

"Um . . . is this Lemonade?"

"Yeah?" I say.

"It's Mei Cunningham."

"Oh, hi, Mei," I tell her. "I mean, *ni hao.*"

"Wow, you remembered!" She laughs. "That's really good!"

"Thanks!" I say.

"We were wondering if you wanted to come and play Kick the Can today. We're all getting together at Nick French's house again. Me, Eliza Rose, J-Man, Joe Kelly, and Beau."

"Oh," I say, looking over at Tobin.

He's eyeing me suspiciously over his yellow legal pad.

"Um . . . I'm not really sure . . . b-but I don't think I can," I stutter.

"Oh." She sounds disappointed. "Well, if you change your mind, meet us there after lunch. Around one or so."

"Okay," I say. "And thanks."

"See you."

"Bye," I tell her, and slip the receiver back into its cradle. I pick up my book.

"Who was that?" Tobin asks.

"What?" I say without looking up, even though I heard him just fine.

"Who was that?"

"Mei Cunningham," I say. "They're playing Kick the Can at Nick French's house and invited us to come."

That's not exactly a lie. I mean, technically *I* was invited. Mei just didn't mention anything about Tobin. He's too smart for me, though.

"Clarification—they invited *you.*" He points in my direction and goes back to shuffling his yellow papers.

"Well, you could go too. If you wanted to, you could."

"Oh, yeah? Who says?"

"I say."

"Why would I want to play with those guys, anyway?"

"Why not?"

"Because," he says.

"'Because' isn't a reason. Is it just because of the prank calls?"

"No, it's not just the prank calls."

"The girlfriend cracks?"

"No, not just the girlfriend cracks either."

"Well, it seems to me that nothing is that big of a deal that you can't try and make friends with them. You go to the same school and all."

"That's not my choice," he says. "I don't do anything to them."

"Yeah, but you can still try to change it."

"Yeah, well, if you were the one who had dodgeballs whipped at your head every day at recess since kindergarten, you might not feel that way," he mumbles.

"What?"

He doesn't look at me.

"They whip balls at your head?"

"Only every day," he says.

"What else?"

"They call me names."

"Names?"

"Mean ones, too."

The more he tells me, the more it makes my volcano bubble up, not for me . . . but for him.

"Every day since kindergarten?" I ask.

"Minus weekends and major holidays," he says.

"I didn't know it was that bad."

"And then there was the time they locked me in the girls' room."

"Are you kidding me?" I ask. "That's it." I slam my book closed. "We're going."

"But, Lemonade—"

I hold up my hand.

"Remember when I told you I was going to teach you a thing or two about standing up to those guys?"

He nods.

"Well, school's in session."

He looks at me, confused.

"School doesn't start for another fourteen days," he tells me.

"What? No . . . never mind. Let's just go."

"Go where?" he asks.

"You'll see."

• • •

In Tobin's bedroom that afternoon, it's an all-out wrestling brawl.

"You can wear it when we get back!" I yank on his safari hat, still strapped tight under his chin.

He sits in the middle of his bedroom floor, clutching the brim with both hands, gripping as tight as his fingers will hold it.

"I'm not taking it off, and you can't make me!" he screams, like he's two years old instead of ten and a half.

He doesn't know it yet, but he doesn't stand a chance, since I'm two whole inches taller and way stronger. And soon it comes loose and it's mine.

"Fine!" He rubs at the rug burns on his knees. "You'll see how it is, and then you'll be sorry you ever made me go."

"I'm just asking you to give it a chance. That's all I'm asking," I say.

"Uh-huh," he grumbles.

•  •  •

Tobin and I ride to Nick French's that afternoon. Me on my pink-and-green bike, and Tobin safari hat–free. Which is nothing short of a miracle. Well, mostly miracle, and only a little bit of force.

Joe Kelly is the first one to spot us riding up the street.

"Hey, it's Tobin Sky and his *girlfriend*!" he hollers at us with a big, stupid grin.

The other kids come out of their hiding spots underneath bushes and behind trees, where they were perched to try to steal the can from the person who's It in back of the house. The can again being the dirty orange Nerf football.

Beau laughs at the girlfriend comment and so does J-Man.

"Leave him alone, you guys!" Eliza Rose says, peeking out from under a tall green bush. "Hi, Lemonade! The kitties are almost ready to go! You ask your grandfather yet?"

I shake my head.

"Not yet," I call back.

Mei Cunningham must have lost at Inka Binka Bottle of

Ink and must be out back guarding the coveted orange foam trophy.

"Tobin and his *girlfriend* want to play Kick the Can," Beau chimes in. "How romantic!"

"If you need any tips, just let me know," Tobin says like a pro while he puts his kickstand down in the driveway.

J-Man and Nick French burst out laughing.

"Dude, burn! He got you good." J-Man points at Beau and laughs harder.

Joe Kelly and Beau don't laugh.

"What did you say to me?" Beau demands, puffing up his chest and looking down his nose at Tobin.

Tobin sneaks a look at me, and I nod at him.

"I said, if you need any tips, just let me know," Tobin says again, looking Beau straight in the eye.

"What's that supposed to mean?" Joe Kelly asks.

"It means . . . ah . . . that I have a, ah . . . it means if you can't . . . me and Lemonade . . . um—"

So close.

"Look." I step in, pointing my finger at Beau's chest. "Here's the deal: If I hear another thing about dodgeballs or the girls' bathroom, or if I pick up the receiver and hear your stupid voice screeching over the phone, you're going to have me to deal with. Do we understand each other? And his name is Tobin, get it?" I poke Beau. "I don't want to hear about you calling him anything else."

"Yeah." Tobin mimics me, putting his hands on his hips and looking fierce. As fierce as you can look with beads of sweat on your upper lip.

"And just so you know, we're both playing, so get over it."

Joe Kelly is staring at me with a smile.

"Fine," he says. "You want Tobin to play, he can play. I don't have a problem with that. He's with you, he's okay in my book."

"Well, good," I say. "It's settled, then."

Beau crosses his arms, swings the bangs out of his face, and glares at Tobin, while Tobin suddenly finds his feet extremely fascinating.

"Hey." Mei comes around the side of the house from the back. "Where did everyone go?"

Nick French's face turns Maraschino Red.

"Lemonade is here!" Eliza Rose announces.

"Oh, hey, Lemonade! I'm glad you decided to come. Hi, Tobin." Mei smiles and waves. "So, what's the holdup? I don't want to be It forever, you know. Let's play."

Everyone darts in different directions to hide.

"You okay?" I whisper to Tobin.

He wipes the sweat beads off his face.

"I think they still hate me."

"Give them a chance to change," I say. "To see what I see."

"I'm telling you, the war isn't over just 'cause you brought me here."

"Well, maybe it's not the end of the war, but we won a small battle, and sometimes it's the small battles that lead you to victory."

"You know what?" he says.

"What?"

"That actually sounds very lemonade-ish."

I smile.

"Yeah?"

"Yeah," he says. "Maybe you're starting to remember what you think you forgot."

"Maybe I am," I say.

# 41

# A NEST

"But, Mrs. Dickerson . . . ," Tobin starts. "Yes, but . . . yes, Mrs. Dickerson . . . I . . . what? You made the peanut butter ones?"

He looks at me.

*Come on*, I mouth, pointing to the hands on his Bigfoot watch. *We're . . . going . . . to . . . be . . . late.*

He puts his hand over the green receiver.

"She had another sighting and made the peanut butter ones."

"Polaroid?" I ask.

"Mrs. Dickerson?" Tobin says. "Uh-huh . . . Mrs. Dickerson? Did you . . . did you get a picture?"

He looks at me and shakes his head, then listens some more.

"You found a *what*?" he asks. "Really? Roofed or unroofed?"

His eyes find mine again and they're wider than I've ever seen them.

He covers the receiver again. "She found a nest," he whispers.

• • •

After Tobin finally hangs up, we lock up shop and race our bikes through town to Mr. Harold's ranch. Tobin set up a daytime expedition and some of the kids agreed to come along.

Yesterday wasn't perfect, but anything's better than a dodgeball to the head. And that's a good place to start.

"So, what do the nests look like?" I shout over to him.

He's pedaling fast on his fire-engine-red bike, with the black leather case and yellow legal pad strapped over the rear wheel.

"They're very intricate," he hollers back. "And there's no way an animal without opposable thumbs could create one. Branches are intertwined, and some have roofs and others don't. She says this one has a roof."

"Where did she see it?"

"Just past the tree line back by her garden. She thinks a Bigfoot has been stealing the vegetables from her garden and stashing them in the nest."

"But no Polaroid?"

"Nope," he says. "But she's positive she can see the structure through the branches."

"Do the Bigfoot eat vegetables?" I ask.

"Of course, what do you think they eat?"

"Actually, I worried that it might be ten-year-old girls."

Tobin snorts.

"None that I've ever heard of. They're omnivores, so they eat food of both plant and animal origin."

"Animal origin?"

"In addition to vegetation and berries, animal meat. Deer. Squirrel. Stuff like that."

"What else?" I ask.

"What do you mean, what else? Like Twinkies or something?"

I laugh.

"I would bet you a million dollars no Bigfoot in its right mind would eat a Twinkie. They only eat real food," he says.

"Twinkies are real."

"They are not. They don't grow on a Twinkie tree."

"Well, they're still real. You can see them. They exist."

"Okay, fine, they exist, I'll give you that one. But what in Sam Hill is so great about them, anyway?"

I think about it.

"It's got to be the cake-to-filling ratio," I tell him.

"The what?" He looks over at me.

"The snack-cake-to-filling ratio. It's always perfect. Just enough filling to go with every cakey bite. You never have too much filling or too much snack cake. The wrong ratio will ruin your dessert every time."

An exaggerated blast of air blows up the brim of his safari hat, telling me we're done with the whole conversation about Twinkies or any Twinkie-eating Bigfoot.

"So, are we going to check it out? Mrs. Dickerson's sighting, I mean."

"Yeah, after this. There they are." He points to the others waiting at Mr. Harold's iron gate.

There's three of them. Joe Kelly, Eliza Rose, and Beau Stitch.

"It's only about one hundred degrees out here, Bigfoot hunter," Beau hollers at us, swinging his bangs. "Are we doing this, or what?"

"Guess what?" I say to Eliza Rose, putting my kickstand down in the dirt with the tip of my tennis shoe. "We got a call from Mrs. Dickerson, and she thinks a Bigfoot is actually eating the vegetables out of her garden!"

"No way!" Eliza Rose says.

"Yep."

"Are we going to sit around here yakking, or what?" Beau complains.

"Yeah, what's the plan, Tobin?" Joe Kelly asks.

"Mr. Harold said he'd meet us at the house," Tobin says. "Let's head there and then decide how we're going to do it once we get to the woods."

We saddle back up on our bikes and pedal up the long dirt drive toward Mr. Harold's white farmhouse. The steers on either side chew long blades of grass and stare at us from behind the weathered fencing.

They chew and stare.

Stare and chew.

I wonder what they're thinking about today. When I look at Tobin, he just shakes his head.

"They wouldn't eat the Twinkies either, so don't even start," he says before I can even open my mouth.

I laugh out loud.

"Then I'll just say this, I bet they'd love them too!"

He just rolls his eyes.

Mr. Harold is sitting on the porch steps drinking an icy bottle of RC Cola when we get there.

"Hello!" he calls out to us with a wave. "Back for more exploring, are you? You picked a much better day for it. Hot, but at least it isn't storming."

"Hi, Mr. Harold," I call back, parking my bike next to his blue Ford pickup.

"Hello, Lemonade." He takes another sip of the RC, then wipes the back of his neck with the red bandana. "I see you brought along reinforcements."

"This is Eliza Rose, Joe Kelly, and Beau Stitch."

"Pleasure." Mr. Harold nods. "What's on the agenda?"

"We were just hoping to get out past the fence where you said you saw that Bigfoot and do some more investigating," Tobin tells him.

"You have permission to go out past the fence today?"

"Yes, sir," Tobin says. "Uh . . . you know . . . *daytime* permission."

"Ahhh . . . well, that sounds good to me." Mr. Harold smiles. "I'll be out in the pasture tending to the steers if you need me. Just holler."

"Thanks, Mr. Harold," Tobin says, untying his case from the back of his bike. "Okay, everybody, we're burning daylight. Let's get a move on."

When we make it to the fence where Mr. Harold said he saw something, Tobin sets down the case.

"Let's break up into two groups," he says, unzipping the case and pulling out the Polaroid.

"I'm going with Lemonade," Eliza Rose announces, linking arms with me.

I turn to her, and she smiles. It feels nice to be making friends here like I had back in San Francisco.

"How about you boys go your way and we go ours?" I say. Everyone agrees.

"Lemonade, you are assigned to still pictures." Tobin hands me the Polaroid camera.

I nod and pull the strap over my head.

"I've got movie camera duty," he continues. "Joe, me, and Beau will head east. Lemonade, you and Eliza Rose can head west. We are looking for evidence of any kind. Footprints, hair, scat."

"What's scat?" Eliza Rose whispers to me.

"I'll tell you later," I whisper back.

Eliza Rose raises her hand. "What if we see something?" she asks. "I mean, what if we come across an actual Bigfoot?"

"They're mostly nocturnal, but there's always a chance. Take a picture first and foremost. That's very important. Always a picture first. Let me hear you all say it."

They all look at each other.

"I don't hear anything," Tobin tells them, putting a hand to his ear.

"Always a picture first," we drone in unison.

"We'll also need a special call, you know, in case we see something. To signal the other group."

"How about *whoooo-hoooo*?" Eliza Rose suggests, standing on her tiptoes and waving her arm in the air.

"No way," Joe Kelly says. "A whistle." He sticks two fingers in his mouth and lets out a loud screech.

"I'm not going to slobber all over myself to whistle like that." Eliza Rose puts her hands on her hips.

"It's easy," Joe tells her. "You just wet these two fingers, roll your tongue, and—"

"How about an owl call, like this." Beau cups his mouth with his hands and makes the sound of an owl. *"Hooo-hooo!"*

"What's the difference between that and what I said?" Eliza Rose demands.

"Well, one is a shrill little-girly call, and the other is a wild-bird call. There's a big difference," Beau says.

"Okay, okay." I hold up my hands. "The call will be one short *whooop*. Like this." I cup my hands around my mouth. *"Whooop!* Like that. *Whooop!"*

The *whooop* puts an end to the whole debate, and everyone nods in agreement. Tobin looks at his Bigfoot watch and holds it up to his ear.

"It is thirteen hundred hours. We will meet back here at exactly fifteen hundred hours to debrief, and not a minute later." He looks right at me and then winds the small silver knob on his watch. "Should we go ahead and synchronize?" he asks, squinting down at his arm, still messing with the knob.

Joe looks at Beau, and Beau looks at Eliza Rose, and Eliza Rose looks at me.

Silence.

Tobin looks up at all of us.

"Well?"

More silence.

"What's he talking about now?" Eliza Rose finally whispers in my direction.

# 42

## OPERATION: MR. HAROLD'S RANCH, PART TWO

"And he really thinks it's monkey hair?" Eliza Rose says as we trudge through tall grasses and push past long pine arms.

"Half primate and half human," I say.

"That's crazy." She wipes sweat off her forehead. "Oh, and what's scat, anyway?"

"You don't want to know," I say, stepping over a large boulder.

"Sure I do."

I turn back to face her. "It's poo."

She stops. "Okay, I didn't want to know that."

"I told you so," I laugh, sitting down on top of the rock.

I sneeze and wipe my nose with my forearm.

"We should have brought a canteen of water," Eliza Rose says, leaning up against the trunk of a tall oak. "You think Mr. Harold would let us have one of his bottles of RC Cola to share?"

"Maybe," I say.

"How much longer are we going to do this?" She yawns. "It's so hot, and *Scooby-Doo!* starts at three o'clock. It's the one where Scooby and Shaggy get locked in the basement on an old abandoned farm. I read it in the *TV Guide*."

"We'll stay until we find some evidence. Plus, I saw that one already. It's a rerun."

"I know, but it's funny," she says, fanning herself. "And don't you think Fred is cute?"

"He's a cartoon."

"Still," she says. "When I get married, I want my husband to look just like him."

"Let's keep going," I say. "We have to find something or—"

Eliza Rose gasps.

"What was that?" she whispers.

"I don't know," I whisper back.

I crouch low behind a thick bush and scan the forest through the Polaroid's viewfinder, my finger on the red button, ready to click. Eliza Rose scrambles over near me, linking her arm with mine.

"Was it a branch cracking?" I ask her.

"Sounded more like someone cracking a stick against a tree," she says.

I scan the forest again, but all I see through the lens is green.

"Oh, no!" she whispers.

"What?"

"Now I can't remember what we decided the call is supposed to be! Was it the owl or the whistle? And what if it's hungry?"

"It's okay," I say. "They eat mostly vegetation, anyway."

That's not really a lie.

"What does *mostly* mean?"

"The call is the *whooop*, remember?"

"Oh, yeah, that's right, the *whooop*," she says. "Should I do it now? Should I *whooop* now?"

"Wait," I say, squinting through the viewfinder.

Still just green.

Green leaves.

Green moss.

Green bushes.

"Now?" she says again.

"Not yet," I whisper.

We crouch in silence, listening to the sounds of the woods. The wind blowing through the tops of the trees makes a *shhhhh* sound. The birds up above us call back and forth. And far out in the pasture, we hear the low moan of steers complaining about the sun.

"I don't hear anything now, do you?" I whisper.

"No."

"*Whooop, whooop!*"

We turn to each other with our mouths open and our eyes wide.

"Was that—?"

"Yeah!" I say. "Come on!"

We jump up and dart in the direction where we last saw the boys.

• • •

After four rounds of *whooops*, we spot the three of them huddled under the bottom bough of a pine tree that has a trunk thicker than the three of them standing side by side.

"What are you doing under there?" I call out.

"Shhh!" Tobin hisses, motioning for us to hurry.

Eliza Rose and I scramble over rocks and old fallen needles and branches to reach them. When we do, we huddle under the pine branches too. It smells like Christmastime under there.

Pine needles and bark and sap.

*Something is following us*, Tobin mouths to us, peering over his wire-rims and pointing to the left.

"You're lying," Eliza Rose says, frantically scanning the woods.

"Something really is following us," Joe Kelly whispers. "Something big, too."

That's when Eliza Rose starts bawling.

"*Ohhhh*," she whines. "I don't want to be eaten by a Bigfoot."

"I told you they're mostly vegetarian, didn't I?" I say.

"Is *mostly* the same as *all*?" she asks.

"No."

"Then I want out of here right this second," she says.

"For criminy sake," Tobin says. "You're going to scare whatever it is off."

"Good!" Eliza Rose sniffs. "Lemonade, let's go. I don't want to do this anymore."

"I'll take her back," I tell them.

"I'll go with her," Beau says, stuffing his hands in his pockets and flipping his bangs.

"Yeah . . . me too," Joe Kelly says. "You know, it's so hot and everything . . . maybe we could do it again when it cools down a little. Like October. October sounds good. Everyone good for October?"

I look at Tobin, and he looks at me, and then he rolls his eyes so hard I think they're going to fall right out of his head.

"Hey! You! You there! Stop!"

A loud gunshot blast fires, making my ears ring.

"Move, move, move!" Tobin yells.

He pushes everyone out of his way and darts out from under the pine tree and through the forest like a rocket. The rest of us scramble to keep up with him.

When we make it to the wooden fence, I climb on top of it and shield my eyes from the sun with my hand. Mr. Harold is on Cimarron out in the west field at the edge of the fence. He has his rifle in his hand pointed straight upward.

"Mr. Harold!" Tobin hollers, waving his arm. "What are you doing?"

Mr. Harold flips the reins and kicks the sides of Cimarron's fat brown belly. "Yah!" he yells, and the horse begins to gallop in our direction. When they reach us, Mr. Harold jumps off.

"Was it a Bigfoot?" I ask.

"Why do you have a rifle, Mr. Harold? They won't hurt you," Tobin says.

"I think someone or something ran off with one of my

chickens. One was missing yesterday, too, but I thought it just wandered off or a dog got to it." Mr. Harold keeps scanning the woods. "Just now, I saw something running through the forest with another one of my chickens under its arm."

"What do you think it was?" Joe Kelly asks.

"Was it a biped, Mr. Harold?" Tobin asks.

Mr. Harold turns his head to face Tobin and then forces a smile.

"You know what? It was probably just someone down on their luck . . . looking for a meal. I don't know who it was. And he's gone now, so . . . so let's get you Bigfoot hunters an ice-cold RC Cola. You could probably use it."

# 43

# THE MYSTERY OF
# THE GIANT PUMPKIN

"And then they *all* wanted to go home," Tobin tells Mrs. Dickerson, biting into a buttery ear of corn. "Right in the middle of the doggone expedition!"

Mrs. Dickerson sips her tea. "Is that so?"

"It is so. And that's the very reason why I don't have anyone else in my Inc." Tobin wipes butter off his lips with his arm and takes another juicy bite.

"Well, I guess that's why God sent you, Lemonade." Mrs. Dickerson winks at me.

"I guess," Tobin agrees. "I mean, she's got the sneezing and has dumb questions sometimes, and there's all those Twinkie breaks, but at least she's no chicken."

I laugh, which makes me snort, which makes the milk I'm drinking spray out of my nose.

"I'm so glad that there is some sort of friendship growing

with the others," Mrs. Dickerson says, handing me another napkin. "My guess is Lemonade had something to do with that, too."

"Yeah, she schooled me," Tobin says, taking another bite.

"Pardon me?"

"It means Lemonade is good at making friends . . . and also at comebacks. She says she's going to make me into the Comeback King." He looks at me, and we both laugh.

"Let's not get crazy," I tell him.

"Comeback King?" Mrs. Dickerson pronounces each word very carefully, like she's speaking Swahili for the first time, which makes Tobin and me laugh even harder.

"It doesn't matter," I tell her. "Tobin said you think you found a nest out back."

"Oh, my, yes!" Mrs. Dickerson takes the cloth napkin that she keeps tucked in her lap and dabs the corners of the bright pink lipstick that never seems to want to stay where it's supposed to. Then she leans forward on her elbows. "I'm sure it's a Bigfoot nest—sure as I'm sitting here, that's what it is."

"Roofed, right?" Tobin blurts out, spitting corn kernels on the yellow tablecloth.

"Yes, definitely roofed . . . and inside it . . ." She leans even farther forward and raises her eyebrows. "A soft pile of leaves on top of pine needles and branches."

"You mean like a bed?" I ask.

"That's exactly what I mean," Mrs. Dickerson says. "Not only that, but in the corner, there are piles of vegetables straight from my garden. Mind you, I only saw it from a distance."

"So how can you tell they're yours?" I ask her.

Mrs. Dickerson looks me straight in the eye.

"A gardener knows, dear."

"Oh," I say.

"I've been missing vegetables for some time now, but of course I just figured it was the rabbits, you know. From time to time, I'm chasing those pesky little guys away with my cane. But today . . . today"—she points her finger in the air—"was different."

"Why?" Tobin asks.

"Because today I found an *entire* pumpkin gone."

"An *entire* pumpkin?" I repeat.

"That's right. And not just any pumpkin, one that was at least fifteen pounds. Much too big for a rabbit . . . or any other critter in the forest, for that matter. I was waiting to see just how big it would grow before Halloween rolled around. I thought I could carve a nice jack-o'-lantern out of it, you know, to put on the front porch when trick-or-treaters come—"

"How big was it?" Tobin asks.

"Well, I suppose enough to freeze a couple of pies for Thanksgiving and a few pans of roasted seeds for snacking."

"No, Mrs. Dickerson . . . ," Tobin says. "The nest. How big is the nest?"

"Oh, yes, well, it's big enough."

"Big enough for what?" I ask.

"Big enough for more than one of them," she says.

"Well, I can see why the Bigfoot is stealing your vegetables, Mrs. Dickerson," I tell her, looking down at the gnawed corncobs on my plate.

"Oh, my Lemonade, aren't you a sweet girl!" she exclaims, putting her hands on her cheeks. "The spitting image of your mother, I'm telling you! Just the spitting image."

*Elizabeth Lilly Witt.*

Except this time when I hear about Mama and say her name inside my head, there's no lump to swallow down.

I smile instead.

No volcano bubbling up.

No quicksand sucking me in.

Not that I don't still wish that Mama was here having dinner at Mrs. Dickerson's with us right this minute. Or that I could tell her all the things I've been doing in Willow Creek. Or that I could see her and Charlie make things right between them. Or even that I could smell her strawberry Suave.

But for the first time since she's been gone, I don't feel like I'm drowning or bubbling lava, or holding something way too heavy for me to carry. Here, in Willow Creek . . . I feel found.

Found by a new kind of family.

And I know it's Mama who got me here.

# 44

# OPERATION: MRS. DICKERSON'S GARDEN

Mrs. Dickerson's backyard is small, with a heavy forest of pines lined right up against the end of her gardens. She has two gardens out back, one that's all vegetables and one that's all flowers.

On our way out the kitchen door to investigate the mystery of the missing pumpkin, Tobin pulls the two cameras and two flashlights from his case.

"Here." He hands me one of the flashlights and the Polaroid.

I slip the camera strap over my head.

"Remember, picture first, always picture—"

"I know, I know," I say.

Tobin slips the movie camera's strap around his neck and double-checks the chin strap on his safari hat.

"Ready?" he asks. "Flashlights . . . check."

"Check," I tell him, flipping my switch.

"Check." He flips his.

"Cameras ready . . . check."

"Check," I say.

"Check," he says.

"Let's examine the garden first," Tobin says then. "It's nineteen hundred hours already, and Charlie said to leave Mrs. Dickerson's by nineteen-thirty."

"Right," I say.

We investigate up and down all the rows between the pumpkin vines, carrot tops, tomato plants, and carefully lined-up herbs, all labeled with tiny handwritten signs.

Rosemary
Carrots
Tomatoes
Green Beans

"There are so many dents in the dirt, it's hard to tell who's been in here," he says.

"Here's where the pumpkin must have been," I say, crouching down near an empty green vine. I hold it up for him to see.

"But you know what?" I look at it closer. "It looks like it's been cut . . . like with a knife, not gnawed with teeth."

Tobin steps over Mrs. Dickerson's carefully planted rows of greens and reaches down to grab it. He examines it close, running a finger over the clean cut. He checks his watch again.

"Take a picture," he says.

I aim the Polaroid in the direction of the vine and snap a shot.

"Let's head to the tree line to see if we can find the structure," he says. "We're running out of time. We can always come back and examine this more tomorrow. I want to see that nest."

I follow him. Inside the woods, it's already dark, even though the sun isn't quite down yet. The pines reach toward the sky, hiding their deepest secrets. We turn on our flashlights and step over small bushes and push past long pine arms, just beyond the tree line.

"There it is!" Tobin hollers, shining his light on some twigs tied together into some kind of hut.

"That's it?"

"Yeah, right there." He points. "See it? See the braiding of the tree branches? It's spectacular!"

When we reach it, I examine the outside, taking Polaroids to document the find. It's a tall structure with a doorway, and broken twigs are wound together like braids to make walls and a roof. Pine branches cover the top of it, which almost makes it invisible in the woods, unless you're actually looking for it.

We stop at the doorway and look at each other.

"You go first," I tell him.

He takes a deep breath. He peeks around the edge of the doorway, shining light inside.

"All clear," he calls back.

I peek around the corner too and shine my light inside.

"The pumpkin!" I exclaim, pointing to it in the corner of the nest.

"Look over here." Tobin shines his flashlight next to a bed made out of pine needles. "A pile of newspapers."

"Newspapers?" I say, peering over his shoulder. "Don't even try to tell me the Bigfoot reads the *Two Rivers Tribune*."

"Look at this, too . . . clothes." Tobin grabs a camouflage sweatshirt off the ground.

"What's that?" I aim my light toward a small wooden box stuffed between the pine-needle bed and the stack of newspapers.

Tobin takes a step closer and reaches down to pull it out. It's got curling vines carved all over it. On the top, bottom, and sides, too.

"Open it," I tell him.

Tobin lifts the lid and peers inside.

"Well?" I ask. "What's in there?"

Tobin doesn't say anything.

I peek over the lid myself. "Is that a picture?" I ask, shining my light on it.

"Yeah," Tobin says.

"A picture of what?"

"It—it's . . . a . . . it's a, um—" Tobin stammers, staring down at it.

"It's a what?"

Tobin peers over his wire-rims at me but doesn't say a word. Not one single word.

I reach over the lid and grab the photo from the box.

"Oh," I say, sucking in my breath and swallowing hard. "Tobin," I whisper. "It's you."

# 45

# SECRETS IN THE PINES

"I—I must have dropped it," he stammers, starting to pace the length of the nest. "That day we were out here dusting for prints. Or you did, maybe. That's got to be it."

"It's the same one, right? The one in your case? Is yours missing?"

"I—I don't know. It must be."

"Go and check," I say.

"Yeah, okay. You come with me."

That's when we hear the footsteps.

Running footsteps.

"Turn your light out," Tobin whispers. "Turn it off! Hurry up!"

While I fumble with the switch, he grabs my arm and pulls me low to the ground, near the pile of old newspapers. The footsteps are coming closer, pounding the dirt, cracking sticks and grinding rocks into the earth.

Hard.

Fast.

A large body smashing through leafy branches.

Tobin's breathing is heavy, and his face is close to mine. His breath smells like Mrs. Dickerson's hot buttered corn. My heart is beating so loud, I'm sure he can hear it banging against my chest.

The footsteps get louder and louder, until we can hear the snapping of twigs and the swaying of branches right outside the nest.

Then they stop. And he fills the doorway, with heavy breath and darting eyes.

But it's not a Bigfoot.

It's a man. Just a man. A wild man with long, matted reddish-brown hair.

At first he doesn't see us, but when he does, he almost drops the eggs he's holding tight in his fists.

"What—what are you doing in here?" he demands. Sweat is soaking his temples and his tan T-shirt. "Where—"

My hands are shaking while I fumble to turn my flashlight back on. I shine it in his direction, and then he does drop the eggs while he tries to cover his face with his arms. Like we're grizzly bears lying in wait, ready to eat him for dinner.

"No—please!" he begs.

He's dirty and he stinks something awful. Like he hasn't seen a Mr. Bubble bath *or* a bar of Irish Spring in a long time. His reddish-brown hair is scraggly, with a matching beard hanging down to his chest all tied up in knots. He's wearing camouflage pants, and his shirt is ripped across one shoulder, and there are holes in the front. He peers out at us from behind his arms, eyes darting like he's a wild deer ready to run from a hunter.

Tobin aims his light on the man now too.

"Please state your name and business here, sir," Tobin demands, his voice shaking.

"I—I—" the man starts. "Tobin, please! I can't—"

That's when I hear Tobin make the same weird sound in his throat he made that day at the store when the boys came in to hassle him. He slowly lowers the flashlight to his side.

"What did you say?" he asks.

"Please . . . just leave me be. You need to leave here—"

"Do you know me?" Tobin asks him. "Did you take this?" He holds out the picture. "Because this is mine . . . did you steal this from me?"

"Let's just go." I grab Tobin's arm and start to pull. "He wants us to leave."

"It's not yours," the man says then.

"What do you mean, it's not mine? It *is* mine. It's me and it's my dad. This is mine. Not yours. How dare you steal it from me? How dare you . . . ?"

And then Tobin stops. He doesn't say anything more. He doesn't breathe or move or anything. He just stands frozen, like the wooden Bigfoot statue in the center of town.

Except for one part of him. The picture in his hand starts to shake.

"Tobin," I say again. "Please, let's just go."

"Wait," Tobin says, raising the flashlight one more time toward the man and then looking at the picture in his hand.

"He told us to go, let's just go," I say.

"But I think . . . I think I know who it is," he whispers.

Tobin takes a step forward.

"You do?" I ask.

"Is it . . . is it you?" he asks the wild man. His voice comes out all high and garbled.

The man hesitates. He turns, his eyes skimming the forest behind him, wondering where to run. Where to hide. Then he slowly lowers his arms, and then his head, and then his shoulders, like he's surrendering to the hunters who have cornered him.

Defeated.

"Tobin," I demand. "Who *is* that?"

He doesn't take his eyes off the man.

We all three just stand in silence. The picture in Tobin's hand is still shaking.

"Tobin?" I finally say again. "Who—"

"Lemonade." He turns to me and whispers, "I think . . . it's my dad."

• • •

"Kids!"

It's Mrs. Dickerson calling us from her back door.

"It's getting too dark now! Come on back!"

"Your dad?" I breathe.

Tobin nods, his eyes glued on the man.

"What are you doing out here?" Tobin asks him.

"Son," the man says, swallowing hard. "I can't believe it . . . you're standing right here . . . right in front of me."

"Right here?" Tobin says. "I've been here the *whole time.*

Where have *you* been? We've been waiting for you to come home. Me and Mom. We thought you were dead."

The man takes a deep breath.

"I've been here. But I couldn't—" he starts. "I can't—"

"How did you know it was me?"

"I've been watching you . . . your mom, from the woods. I couldn't—"

"Watching us? What do you mean? Did you forget where the house is or something?"

"Kids!"

The man jumps, and his eyes scan the darkness.

"Are you there?" Mrs. Dickerson's voice is closer now.

"You can't tell her!" the man whispers at us, moving back and forth in the doorway like a caged animal.

Then he lunges forward into the nest and huddles in a ball on the corner of the pine bed, peeking out between the braided branches. Scanning the forest.

"Yeah, Mrs. Dickerson," I call back. "We're coming!"

"Well, hurry now, it's just too dark to be running in the woods. You need to get back to Charlie's. He's already called twice."

"Mrs. Dickerson—" Tobin starts.

"Don't!" the man pleads. "Please . . . please don't say anything. . . . I can't go back . . . I just can't—"

"Why not?" Tobin demands. "I don't get it. Why didn't you just come home? We went to pick you up, you know . . . at the airport. We waited for you. For a long time, we waited. We thought you were . . . we thought . . . What in Sam Hill are you doing out here in the woods all alone?"

"I—I can't leave the woods . . . the forest . . . it's my protection. My home. I can't leave it."

"What are you talking about?" Tobin goes on with his hands on his hips. "Your home is at the house with us! With Mom and with me."

"You don't understand—"

"No, I don't," Tobin says flatly, crossing his arms in front of his chest.

The man's eyes dart again, like he wants to escape but can't remember how to move.

"Mrs. Dickerson!" Tobin hollers.

"Please!" the man begs again.

"Yes, what is it?" Mrs. Dickerson calls from the yard, somewhere real near the tree line.

Tobin hesitates and then shouts, "Call Charlie back! We need him to come right away! And tell him to see if my mom's home from the hospital yet!"

"Why did you do that?" the man asks, tears starting to make muddy rivers down his face. He wraps his arms around his legs and starts to rock.

"Because you need help," Tobin tells him. "And we need you."

"I can't—" the man starts.

"Well, we're not leaving you out here all alone," Tobin says.

The man wipes at his eyes.

"Charlie is on his way!" Mrs. Dickerson's voice announces a minute later. "Is everything all right?"

# 46

# REUNITED

"Lemonade!"

That's Charlie.

His heavy boots pounding the dirt and crunching the leaves and pine needles outside the nest.

"Tobin!" he calls out. "Where are you?"

"Here, Charlie!" I call back. "We're here! In the nest."

More pounding and swatting of branches and crunching ground as Charlie's footsteps get closer and closer. When he appears in the doorway of the nest, he's all out of breath. And he's so tall he has to duck his head to get inside.

"Lem . . . Tob . . . ," he huffs, sounding relieved. "What is . . . where are . . . who . . ." He chokes and sputters, looking down at Scotty still in a ball in the corner.

"Tobin!" It's Debbie coming up behind Charlie, grabbing

his arm and squeezing her head into the doorway. "Lemonade—"

She still has her white nurse's uniform on, her hair still twisted up in a knot under her nurse's cap. Her normally spotless shoes are covered with mud.

"What's going on here?" She pushes her way in past Charlie and rushes to Tobin's side.

She turns him all around in every direction, looking him over top to bottom to make sure he's all in one piece, and then grabs my hand and pulls me close to her like she's guarding us from a wild animal.

"Who is that?" she asks. "Who are you?" she demands.

"Mom . . . ," Tobin whispers. "It's Dad."

Debbie's mouth falls open and she stares hard at Scotty.

"What did you say?"

"It's him, Mom. It's really him. I guess he must've gotten lost or something."

It's quiet again while Debbie watches the man hiding in the corner, his eyes still darting and his body still curled in a tight ball.

"Scotty?" she says real slowly, like she hardly believes her eyes.

He is still a caught animal ready to be slaughtered. Slaughtered up into jerky bits to be bagged and shelved in the FINE CUISINE section of Bigfoot Souvenirs and More.

"Scotty?" Debbie says, louder this time and stepping toward him. "Is it really you?"

Scotty's body ball is so tight now, it looks like he's trying to make himself invisible so we'll all forget he's still sitting in the corner of the nest.

In the beams of our flashlights, we watch his matted red head slowly bob up and then down.

And that's when I see something I will always remember. For my whole life I will remember it.

Debbie rushes toward him in her dirty nurse's dress and muddy shoes, falling down to her knees and wrapping her arms around him with so much love it makes my eyes blur. They blur up even more when I see her thin shoulders shake against him as she cries loud and hard.

I watch her rock him back and forth, the way you might rock a tiny newborn baby snuggled up in a tight swaddle.

"Scotty." She sobs and rocks and rocks and sobs. "My Scotty," she says over and over, kissing his dark muddy cheeks. "My Scotty . . . I love you so much . . . I just love you so much . . . I thought we'd never see you again."

I look over at Tobin and see a whole bunch of tears all stuck up between his cheeks and the bottom of his glasses. Then I look up at Charlie and see tears rolling down and getting caught in his beard.

I wipe my own tears away with my forearm.

We all cry, seeing the love Debbie has for this man she has waited for and prayed for and hoped for. This man she loves with deep-down love.

It reminds me of the time I wrapped my own arms around Mama in the hospital on the very worst day of my entire life. I bet my shoulders shook when her chest stopped moving up and then down. I bet I shook just like Debbie.

Except these tears are different. Hers. Mine. Tobin's. And Charlie's. While we watch her deep-down love.

These tears are happy tears.

With Mama I was trying to hold on to something I had to let go, and Debbie is holding on to something she gets to keep.

No, these are happy tears for sure.

But watching Debbie, Charlie, and Tobin right this second . . . it sure makes me miss Mama. I miss her like something inside me hurts so bad there isn't anything on this earth that could hurt me more. Not a bullet or knife or gangrene or even an insect-related scourge. Right now, I'd give anything to be with Mama like that. One more chance to be able to wrap my arms around her and hold her tight and rock her small, frail body just like Debbie gets to with Scotty.

If somebody gave me that chance again, I'd never let her go. Not ever. And I'd hold on to her just like Debbie is holding on to Scotty. With deep-down love.

And right this minute, when I feel like I'm getting sucked back into sadness quicksand, I look up at Charlie again and then slip my hand into his. The big hand with the special ring on it.

His fingers fold around mine, just like Mama's used to.

And he squeezes my hand tight.

And I squeeze his hand back.

Just in case he has his own quicksand.

## 47

# THANKFUL

It's the middle of the night when we make it home from the hospital in Blue Lake.

Tobin and I waited a long, long time on the bench welded to the wall, until Debbie came to get us for a short visit in Scotty's hospital room.

But not before we scrubbed all the germs from our hands with disinfectant hospital soap and crossed our hearts, promising to only stay for five minutes.

Scotty already looked better. He was all cleaned up, and someone had cut his hair and shaved off his beard to make him look more like the man in the picture next to Debbie's bed and Tobin's too. He had even eaten half a hospital cheese-burger and some of his fries.

I have so many questions, but figure it's best not to ask them until he's well again. Plus Tobin would probably just roll his eyes right out of his head by the time I was done with all my asking.

I don't remember the ride home, because I fell asleep on the front seat of Jake. I wake up when Charlie carries me inside and sets me on top of my bed.

"Charlie," I say, rubbing my eyes.

"It's late, Lem." He pulls off one of my tennis shoes and then the other one. "We can talk more in the morning."

"Why was Tobin's dad living in the woods out back behind Mrs. Dickerson's garden?"

Charlie breathes out long and hard and sits down next to me on the bed.

"He has something called CSR, Lem," he says. "Combat stress reaction. Sometimes it's called battle fatigue or shell shock. It's what some soldiers experience after they must see and do terrible things during a war. Right now he needs rest and he needs some time to make sense of the things he has experienced. He needs help with his memories."

I guess even Scotty has his very own quicksand.

"But why didn't he just go home to get all that?" I ask, thinking about the special ring on Debbie's finger. "Debbie would have helped him. Didn't he know that she has deep-down love for him? Debbie would have done anything he needed. I know it."

"I'm sure you're right about that," Charlie says. "CSR is hard to understand because you can't see it like you can see a broken arm or . . . uh—"

"Gangrene?"

"Yes." He smiles. "Like you can see gangrene. Some people

don't even want to believe CSR is real. But it's very real, and our men need support after all they've been through. All I can say is that Scotty will be okay after he gets treatment at the hospital. He might be there for a time, but the doctors know what to do to help him."

"And he'll be able to go back home one day to live with Tobin and Debbie?"

"Yes, Lem. They can finally be a family again."

"That's good, then," I say.

"Yep." He sighs and stands up. "It's wonderful. Get some sleep now."

"Charlie?"

"Lem, it's late. Crawl in now, and we'll talk more tomorrow," he says, lifting the comforter up for me to burrow under.

"Just one more thing," I tell him, pulling it over my clothes.

"What is it?"

"How did Scotty get all the way from Vietnam back to the woods in Willow Creek?"

He begins tucking the comforter tight all around me.

"Remember when I told you that Scotty had been MIA? Missing in action? And then they rescued him last year?"

"Yes," I say. "I remember. You said he made it to the base in Oakland and then disappeared."

"Yes, well, Scotty told us an amazing story of survival," he tells me. "He had been on a top secret mission when he was captured. His entire squad was killed, but he survived. The army thought they had all been killed, and unfortunately,

Scotty ended up spending the next three years in a prison in the jungle, where he was horribly tortured until another top secret squad finally found him and rescued him last year. That's when they sent soldiers to the house to let Debbie know he was alive. Remember when I told you that Debbie and Tobin went to pick him up at the airport and found out he never made it on the plane?"

"Yes."

"Something happened to him on his way to catch the flight."

"What?" I ask.

"With combat stress reaction, sometimes a person's memories are so strong that it makes them uncertain if a memory is something that happened in the past or if it's happening in the present."

"Kind of like a dream?" I ask, thinking of all the dreams I have of Mama and me at Sunshine's on the Bay. It feels so real when it's happening that it's like she's still right here with me.

"Exactly," he says. "It was the loud noises at the airport that confused his brain. Loud noises that sounded like the explosions or gunfire he experienced in the jungle. Those noises confused him and it's like he started to dream that he was back in the jungle again . . . back in danger. So he did what he learned to do to stay safe. He escaped to the cover of the woods."

"That's why he didn't get on the plane? Because his memories were confused?" I ask.

"That's right."

"But he looked okay to me when we saw him in the hospital."

"It's something that comes on a bit unexpectedly. It could still happen if he experiences something that reminds him of the jungle. Does that make sense?"

"I suppose so," I say. "But I still don't know why he wouldn't just let Debbie know all that. Did he forget about her deep-down love?"

"He told the doctors that once he made it back to Willow Creek on his own, he couldn't face Debbie and Tobin. He said he tried many times to make it up those front porch steps, but he couldn't do it. He said that he just couldn't share with them what he had been through because it was too horrible. He wanted to protect them from all that he had seen and experienced out in the jungle so they wouldn't have to experience it too. So . . . he watched over them from the woods, hoping one day he would be able to be with them again."

I think hard about everything Charlie has told me.

"You're right," I tell him. "That *is* hard to understand."

"Yes," he agrees.

"When will he get to go home for good?"

"That depends on his healing."

"I hope he's healed up soon."

"Me too."

"Charlie?"

"Lem, it's so late."

"One more question. I really promise this time."

"What is it?"

"Scotty didn't say anything about seeing the Bigfoot while he was living out behind Mrs. Dickerson's, did he?"

Charlie smiles. "Nope, he sure didn't."

"Hmmm," I say.

"Good night, Lem."

"Charlie?"

He chuckles. "I'm not going to sleep any time soon, am I?"

"Just one more thing, then I really and truly promise to go to sleep. Cross my heart this time."

"Okay, what is it?"

"I'm happy for Tobin, and Debbie too . . . I am. But it also, well, it doesn't really seem fair."

"Fair?" he asks.

"I mean, first, when he got to even hope that his dad was coming back, I wished I could hope too. You know, that Mama would come back to us too. But now Tobin actually gets his dad back. But Mama is never coming back. I can't even hope for it. And it's just not fair, is all."

Charlie sits back down on the edge of the bed and puts a warm hand on top of my knee.

"I can certainly understand why you feel that way," he says. "And you're right, it isn't fair."

"It doesn't mean I'm bad, to feel like that?"

"No, Lem. Not at all."

"I mean, I'm still happy for them," I say. "I really am. But I'm also sad for me. And for you. Even for Mrs. Dickerson."

Charlie drops his head and sighs.

"I'm happy for them and sad for us too," he says. "I think that's a very normal feeling to have."

I smile at him.

"Thanks, Charlie."

"Good night, Lem," he says.

"Night," I say, snuggling down under my rainbow comforter. I watch him turn off the light and walk toward the door.

"Charlie?"

"Yes, Lem?" He turns back to face me from the doorway, the light from the hall shining on him.

"You are what I'm most thankful for today."

Charlie looks at me for a long time without saying anything, and then clears his throat a bunch of times.

"Lemonade Liberty Witt," he finally says, "you are what I'm most thankful for every day."

# 48

# ALWAYS TOGETHER

Mama and I are at the very best table at Sunshine's on the Bay. The one next to the front window that looks out over the water. We watch all the sailboats and ships going back and forth across the bay and listen to the barking sea lions on the dock nearby.

I have my vanilla ice cream, with a mix of exactly fifty percent hot fudge and fifty percent caramel, and a big fat glob of Marshmallow Fluff, with a spattering of rainbow sprinkles on the side. Mama has her chocolate ice cream with chunks of banana, whipped cream, and a cherry on top.

"Mama," I tell her, "I'm most thankful for having this time with you today. I wish it could be more."

Mama smiles her biggest smile. I gaze at her, trying to memorize everything about her. Her shiny lips and her eyelashes and the dusting of freckles on her nose and cheeks.

"I wish it could be more too, Lemonade. But that's out of our control. I'm thankful I got to be your mama, even if it wasn't for the amount of time I had hoped or planned. And now you have Charlie to take care of you. Charlie and Mrs. Dickerson and Debbie and Mr. Harold and Tobin, too."

"And Scotty," I tell her. "He came back, Mama. Tobin and I found him in the woods."

She closes her eyes and nods slowly. She already knows.

"Take care of each other," she says.

"I wish it was you who came back."

"Me too," she says.

"It's not fair that Tobin gets his dad back and I don't get you. It's just not."

"In life, one thing is for sure," she says. "We don't always get to choose."

"You can say that again."

She smiles.

"Remember that with every loss, something meaningful and very special can blossom . . . if you allow it to."

"What good could possibly come from us not being together anymore?" I ask her.

"It doesn't mean what we've lost isn't still important."

"But what could be good about it?" I ask again.

"I think you already know, sweet Lemonade." She smiles.

Bang. Bang. Bang.

Someone is knocking on the front window.

"Lemonade!"

Bang. Bang. Bang.

"Lemonade Liberty Witt!"

I turn to see Tobin standing on the sidewalk, wearing his Bigfoot safari hat strapped tight under his chin, with his Polaroid camera hanging from his neck. He's peering at me between cupped hands through the painted letters on the window advertising the ice cream special of the month.

TIME TO SQUEEZE THE LEMONS ICE CREAM SUNDAE

"Lemonade!" he calls again. "I've got to talk to you!"

"Mama, please don't leave," I say, turning back to face her. "I want you to stay like Tobin's dad gets to."

"I wish I could," she tells me, standing up. "But remember that I will always be with you . . . in here." She taps my forehead gently. "And in here." She places her palm on my heart.

Bang. Bang. Bang.

"Lemonade!"

My eyes peel open. I'm nose to nose with Rainbow, Mama's worn blue bunny with the battered pink bow. And I know this sounds crazy, but I actually catch Rainbow smiling at me.

Bang. Bang. Bang.

The clock next to the bed reads 6:07 a.m. I squint toward the window.

"Lemonade!" Tobin calls through the glass. "Wake up!"

I pull myself up, still in the clothes I had on last night, and push the blue curtains to one side. Tobin is standing there in his tan safari hat with the strap pulled tight under his chin.

"What is it?" I say.

He motions for me to open the window. The sun is just finding its way toward the sky, while the birds call out like an alarm clock, waking the forest grasses and leaves and trees to announce the new day.

"We're leaving for the hospital, and we're going to be there all day," Tobin says. "You're in charge of the Bigfoot Headquarters today."

"What for?"

"What do you mean, what for?"

"I mean, I thought we solved the whole Bigfoot mystery—"

"Tobin!" Debbie calls from across the street. "We have to get going!"

"Here." Tobin shoves a sheet of lined paper toward me.

"What is it?"

"Instructions."

"I don't need instructions."

"You sure do. The last time I left you alone, you took that to mean go play Kick the Can and eat knuckle sandwiches with Mrs. Dickerson."

"They were finger sandwiches. *Finger.*"

"Take it." He shakes the page at me. "Make sure you follow every step. That means opening up at oh eight-thirty hours on the dot."

"Fine." I grab it.

Tobin adjusts his chin strap and turns to leave.

"Tobin," I say.

He turns back.

"Yeah?"

"I—I wanted to tell you, um . . . that I'm . . . you know, ah, that I'm happy for you. I mean that you . . . that you have your dad back and everything. I'm really happy for you."

Tobin smiles.

"Thanks," he says. "I wish it was true for you, too."

"Yeah," I say. "Me too."

He looks away from me and down at his hands.

"So don't forget now, oh eight-thirty hours and not a second later," he reminds me.

"I won't forget it," I tell him. "And you didn't have to write it down, either."

"Really?" he asks.

"Yeah."

"What do you want to bet you're still going to be late?"

"Nuh-uh, I'll be on time. I promise."

"Uh-huh." He grins.

I watch him walk away with his safari hat still strapped tight under his chin. He turns around one more time to wave and I wave back. And then he's off across the street.

On his way to see his dad.

## 49

# 08:30-ISH
# (BUT DON'T TELL TOBIN)

Open the Bigfoot Headquarters at 8:30 and not a minute later.

Check all messages.

Write all messages on pad marked messages.

Call back any messages.

Don't touch the yellow legal pad! You are not authorized at that level of security clearance.

One hot garage plus zero messages and a Bigfoot mystery that's already been solved with a regular man equals the most perfectly boring day in cryptozoological history. Lucky for me, Charlie brought home another new book for me to read, *Otherwise Known as Sheila the Great*.

The green phone rings and I grab the index card next to the message pad, just in case it's Tobin calling to test me.

"*Good morning . . . ,*" I read. "*And thank you for calling Bigfoot Detectives Inc., serving Willow Creek since 1974. This is Lemonade Liberty Witt, Assistant Bigfoot Detective. How may we help you with your Bigfoot needs today?*"

"Lem, it's Charlie."

"Hi, Charlie." I toss the card to the side.

"Just checking up on you. How's business?"

"Boring. But I'm on chapter eight already of my new book."

"Ah," he says. "How is it?"

"It's a real good one."

"Glad you like it. Say, I'm wondering if you want to come up to the store for lunch. I can call Diesel's for some sandwiches."

My stomach moans just hearing about an egg salad on sourdough.

"Sure."

"Egg salad on sourdough, hold the tomatoes?"

I smile into the receiver.

"Thanks, Charlie."

"See you in a few minutes," he says, and hangs up.

I push the folding chair back from the desk and notice that the top left drawer is open a crack. I grab the handle and pull it all the way open. Inside is the yellow legal pad.

And on the very first page it says,

### PRIVATE—KEEP OUT!!
This means you, Lemonade Liberty Witt!!

I ignore the warning and reach down and peel back the page. On the next sheet is a scribble of a smiling Bigfoot and the corporate logo. I skip to a section in the middle of the pad.

June 2, 1975

Dear Dad,
    I got my first employee today. Her name is Lemonade Liberty Witt. She's from the city and kind of weird but I made her my assistant anyway. I think maybe we might even get to be friends. I wish you were here, Dad. It's hard to be here without you.

                    Forever Your Son,
                    Tobin Sky

I turn another page to the next entry, on June 3, 1975.

Dear Dad,
    Where are you? There are so many things I have to tell you. There are so many things I have to ask you. When are you coming back home? I—

The green phone jingles.

I jump out of my skin and throw the pad inside the drawer, slamming it closed. I know this time for sure it's Tobin checking up on me.

"I didn't see anything!" I ramble into the receiver.

"Uh, hello?" says a man's voice.

"Oh—ah." I fumble to grab the note card. "Um, hello . . . ah, *Good morning . . . ,*" I read. *"And thank you for calling Bigfoot Detectives Inc., serving Willow Creek since 1974. This is Lemonade Liberty Witt, Assistant Bigfoot Detective. How may we help you with your Bigfoot needs today?"*

"Hello, Lemonade. It's Mr. Harold."

"Hi, Mr. Harold." I sit back down at the desk. "Did you hear about Tobin's dad?"

"I sure did hear it," he says. "It's all anyone could talk about this morning at the doughnut shop. Nothing short of a miracle."

"Yeah," I agree. "I hope he gets well soon. Charlie says he has PMS."

"Ah—" He chuckles. "I think maybe he said CSR."

"Oh, right, yeah, that was it. I knew it was a bunch of letters."

"Actually, Lemonade, I didn't call to talk about Scotty."

"You didn't?"

"No."

"Why are you calling, then?"

"I'm calling because . . . I saw him again."

"The man?" I ask.

"No, not the man."

"Who, then?"

He's quiet for a long while.

"Who, Mr. Harold?" I ask. "Who did you see?"

He clears his throat.

"The Bigfoot," he says.

# 50

# OPERATION:
# SOLO INVESTIGATION

"But, Mr. Harold," I say, after swallowing an icy sip of my RC Cola on the top step of his porch after lunch with Charlie, "the mystery was solved. It wasn't a Bigfoot at all. It was Tobin's dad the whole time. He told the doctors he's been living in the woods for a year."

Mr. Harold takes a deep breath and wipes the back of his neck with his red bandana.

"I know it," he says. "But that doesn't explain what I saw out in the woods before, or what I saw again today."

"What did you see?"

"Well, I was tending to another part of the fence in the pasture. And there was that smell, you know, that same skunk smell . . . strong, too. And just when I was thinking maybe it wasn't a skunk, that's when the first rock hit me in the back."

"Just like before?"

"Yep. Then another one."

"Another one?" I say, and take a long drink.

"That's when I stood up and turned around," he tells me. "And I saw them."

The RC Cola goes down the wrong pipe, and I choke. My eyes fill up, and I cough and sputter and spray cola everywhere. Mr. Harold smacks my back a couple of times until I stop coughing.

"*Them?*" I gasp for air. "What do you mean, them?"

"I mean there were two of them. A big one and a little one."

"Just like the footprints we found in Bluff Creek!"

"The two of them were hiding behind tree trunks in the woods just past the fence, so I couldn't exactly see them clearly. Maybe there were more, but I can tell you I saw two Bigfoot-type shapes."

"Then what happened?" I ask, kicking myself for not bringing a notepad to write down the details. I'm never going to hear the end of that one.

"The bigger one growled that same growl where the ground shook underneath me, and then threw one more stone that missed me, and then the two of them ran off. I could see that reddish-brown fur for a while, but they dodged through the trees so fast, it wasn't but a minute until I couldn't see them anymore."

"This is unbelievable!" I say.

He nods in agreement.

"I guess I thought the mystery had been solved."

"I mean, yeah . . . you're probably right. Of course you're right. Maybe it was just a grizzly and a cub," Mr. Harold says, already talking himself out of it. "Or maybe another war veteran with battle fatigue . . . or another guy down on his luck living out in the forest here."

"Or," I say, "maybe it wasn't any of those."

• • •

At least I remembered the Polaroid. And a Twinkie, 'cause Bigfoot hunting is hungry work. It was already squished, with the filling smeared on the plastic, but I've learned to live with a squished Twinkie now and again.

I catch a ride out to the pasture behind Mr. Harold on Cimarron's back. Mr. Harold steers the horse right to the part of the fence where he saw the two Bigfoot this morning.

"I talked to Charlie earlier and he said he'd be on his way as soon as he closed up shop. Sure you don't want to wait?" Mr. Harold asks, helping me down.

"Mr. Harold, I'm a professional," I assure him, puffing out my chest to show him my official badge with the clumped-up Elmer's.

"Ah, well, yes, of course. Whatever or whoever it was is gone now. But there must be some evidence left out there somewhere. If you need anything, I'll be right here working on the fence. You just holler. And don't go too far, either."

"Okay," I say. "I won't."

"And how about a *whooop* now and again, just so I know everything is okay?" he asks.

"Sure." I smile. "I'll *whooop* you every five minutes."

"Thanks." He stands up real straight then and salutes me. "Good luck, Bigfoot hunter."

I salute him back and take another deep breath before I climb over the fence.

Over the fence and on my way to my very first solo Bigfoot investigation. I adjust the neck strap on the camera and then take one more look back at Mr. Harold. He's watching me.

"It'll be okay," I assure him again. "I know what I'm doing."

He smiles. "Oh . . . yeah . . . I know it," he calls after me. "I'll give you a shout once Charlie's here. Just remember the *whooop* until then."

"I will," I say.

Then I begin my journey.

A journey to find a Bigfoot.

# 51

# SKUNK STINK AND
# TEN CROOKED TOENAILS

*"Whooop!"*

That was number thirteen. And thirteen *whooop*s times every five minutes is exactly one hour and five minutes that I've been searching, with nothing to show for it.

I hear Mr. Harold's muffled *whooop* back through the trees. I sigh. I miss Tobin. Tobin and his endless Bigfoot details and his eye-rolling and his aversion to Twinkies. Being a solo expeditioner isn't all it's cracked up to be.

When I get hot and feel like a rest, I crawl under the shade of a large pine. The trunk is fatter than me with both arms straight out at my sides, and the bottom row of needles is nearly three feet from the ground. I sit down cross-legged and dig the Twinkie out of my pocket.

It's pancake-squished now, after being in my shorts for so long. I carefully peel the plastic off the cake, listening to the sounds of the forest.

It's kind of like the city, except not at all. Instead of honking horns, birds sing. Instead of bustling feet, crickets chirp. Instead of Miss Kay practicing for the opera, mosquitoes buzz. And instead of smelling like Mr. Chin's glorious crispy fried egg rolls, it smells like pine and moss and dirt and grass and . . .

Skunk.

Actually, wet skunk.

Wait . . . *skunk?*

I stop chewing and hold my breath. Birds sing. Crickets chirp. Mosquitoes buzz.

And a twig snaps. And branches swing. And footsteps stomp.

And there's skunk stink. Strong skunk stink that's getting worse and worse by the second. I hold my nose and breathe out of my mouth.

Maybe it's Mr. Harold again, coming to search for me. Maybe I forgot to *whooop* enough.

That's it . . . it's got to be Mr. Harold. He was so worried about me going alone.

"*Whooop!*" I call between cupped hands.

"*Whooop!*" I hear from way back at the fence post.

Uh-oh.

Then I hear that howl. The same one we heard in the tent the night we stayed out in Mr. Harold's yard.

*Whooooooooooooo!*

The sound makes me jump so high, I almost drop my Twinkie in the dirt. I sit frozen.

Waiting.

Watching.

Worrying.

Wishing Tobin was sitting here next to me.

And that's when I see feet. Reddish-brown feet.

*Furry* feet.

Just past the cover of the bottom bough of the thick pine.

Great big bare feet with actual toes and black crooked toe-nails.

All ten toes stop in front of me, and the rest of whatever belongs to the feet crouches down and peers at me under the pine branch. This time it's not Mr. Harold. It's not a man, either.

It's not even human.

# 52

# TWINKIE

This can't be happening. It has to be a dream. Tobin is going to wake me up any minute now, banging on my window to tell me I'm late for work again. That he's going to have to put the report in my employee file.

But there is no *bang, bang, bang* on my window telling me Mrs. Dickerson called with a fresh pan of cookies or a new sighting.

I squeeze my eyes shut real tight and then open them again. It's real. It's not a dream. I stare at the creature standing in front of me.

A Bigfoot.

My heart isn't beating.

My eyes aren't blinking.

And my legs have gone completely numb.

I'm sure it's a stroke this time.

A real live Bigfoot, peering in at me, ducked under the pine. A reddish-brown creature holding up the bottom bough of the pine tree, sniffing at me. He wrinkles his nose and sniffs me again. I hope I don't smell like a veggie burger with all the fixings.

He snuffs at me then, like I smell more like boiled Brussels sprouts than a juicy burger, which makes me feel a little better. Then I wonder if the Bigfoot thinks I smell as bad as I think he smells. Even though I took a bath with the blue washcloth and Charlie's bar of Irish Spring. It may not be Mr. Bubble, but it does the trick.

He snuffs at me again. I'm as still as a statue. Unable to move.

And even if my brain did remember what I'm supposed to holler, my voice wouldn't remember how to make the sound come out of my throat. And my fingers certainly don't remember how to aim the Polaroid, or that it's even around my neck.

I stare at him, and he stares at me. He wrinkles his nose again and then sniffs again, and then sneezes.

"Gesundheit," I whisper slowly.

He wrinkles his nose again and cocks his head to the right. He's not nine feet. He's smaller. About my size. Except it's hard to tell for sure, since I'm still ducked under the pine and he's still on his feet and bent down peeking in at me.

I wonder how old he is. Maybe almost eleven, like me, since he's almost the same size.

He smells me again, leaning a bit closer to get an even better whiff. He's probably wondering what I'm doing out here. The same thing occurs to me at this very second.

The Bigfoot examines me, looking at every part of me, and I do the same. His hair is scraggly, just like Charlie described. It's long, too, and hangs down from the arms. The hands are well past his knees, like an ape's. He's bipedal and has black fingernails and brown eyes, and when he opens his mouth, I can see a bright red tongue inside.

I don't know what makes me do it, but I slowly reach my hand out toward the creature.

He backs away, letting go of the branch.

"It's okay," I say.

He snorts in and snuffs out, then takes a step forward again. I bring my arm up higher, until it's stretched out as far toward him as it will reach. Just past the very tips of the needles on the lowest branch of the pine.

On my palm, the pancake-flat golden Twinkie.

An offering of peace.

Of friendship.

Of love.

Because the Bigfoot is part of my new family, and my new life, and he's another reason why Mama led me to this very special place called Willow Creek.

My new home.

I'm here to protect the animals. Just like she would. I'm here to have a family. And to make new memories.

The Bigfoot breathes in and out, snorting and snuffing as he moves closer to my hand.

"It's good," I say, smiling hesitantly. "Sweet. With just the perfect cake-to-filling ratio. I know you probably don't understand that, but believe me, it's real important. You can try it, if you want to. Tobin says you won't eat them, but I know you'll like it."

A hairy reddish-brown arm slowly reaches toward me. I remember what Charlie said about that time he saw the Bigfoot in his headlights. He told me the creature looked more scared of him than he was of it. I don't think it's exactly the same for me, since my heart is beating a million beats a second and the whole stroke thing is happening, but he certainly *looks* just as scared as me.

"It's okay," I tell the creature. "I won't ever hurt you. Mama sent me here to help you."

Fingers reach toward me. Real live Bigfoot fingers with wrinkles on the knuckles, and opposable thumbs with dermal ridges on them.

Just when they touch my hand, a loud *whooop* soars through the air from way back near the fence post. Mr. Harold checking up on me. The Bigfoot jumps and then quickly pulls away like he touched a flame.

"It's okay," I say again, taking a deep breath. "It's okay . . . really, it is."

He takes another big snort in my direction and then snuffs out loudly through his mouth this time, spitting at me. Reddish-brown hairy knuckles reach toward me again.

Slower this time.

Reaching gently until they wrap around the Twinkie, his eyes never once leaving mine.

I watch him hold the Twinkie up to his nose and give it a big long sniff.

No snuff.

Then the bright red tongue slips from his mouth and tastes the sweet cream filling. And when I blink again, the Twinkie is gone. In one giant gulp, the entire thing is gone. And the creature stands there staring at me, chewing the golden snack cake.

I knew it!

Chewing.

Staring.

Snuffing.

That's when I hear more footsteps crunching in the woods. Cracking sticks and swaying branches. I know he hears it too, because he stops chewing. He wrinkles his nose up in the air and sniffs in the direction of the noise. He gives me one last look and then disappears through the trees with silent, lightning-fast grace.

He's gone.

And from under the pine, I see Mr. Harold's cowboy boots and Charlie's hiking boots with knee-high socks walk by me.

"Mr. Harold! Charlie!" I call out to them, scrambling out from under the branch.

They stop, and Mr. Harold bends down to give me his hand.

"Oh, Lemonade." He breathes a sigh. "I didn't hear a *whooop* back. I got worried and called Charlie. Everything okay?"

"You seem to be in one piece," Charlie says, leaning down to brush the dirt from my knees.

"He took it!" I tell them.

"Who?" Mr. Harold asks.

"He . . . he took it!" I say again, pointing toward where the creature ran off through the woods. "Right from my hand." I hold my hand out to show them.

"What are you talking about?" Charlie asks.

"My Twinkie."

They stare at me and then at my empty hand.

"Who did?" Mr. Harold asks again.

I take a giant swallow and lean toward them.

"The Littlefoot," I whisper.

# 53

# LEMONADE

"How could you not have taken a picture?" Tobin demands for the zillionth time in a row.

We're all sitting around Charlie's kitchen table. Me, Debbie, Charlie, and Tobin, that same night after they come home from visiting Scotty at the hospital.

Debbie told us that Scotty is making great progress already, and the doctors think he'll be able to go back home soon. Tobin said he beat Scotty in six out of seven games of checkers, but he thought maybe Scotty let him win some of them.

"I told you." I sigh a loud sigh. "It happened so fast that my brain just stopped working. I—I didn't know what else to do."

"How about snap a Polaroid? Remember? Always a picture first. Always a picture—"

"I know it," I say. "But I already told you, my brain stopped working. It was like I was frozen in my skin."

"So, let me get this straight." Tobin holds his head in his hands. "Instead of taking a picture with the camera hanging from your neck so that Bigfoot Detectives Inc. could go down in cryptozoological history and make a discovery that would be in every science book until the end of time, *you shared your Hostess snack cake.*"

He says the last six words real slow, like he can't believe his ears.

"And you were wrong, too. He did like it," I tell him. "He ate the thing in one gulp. And only a few chews."

Tobin slaps his forehead and shakes his head.

"I can't believe you didn't get a picture," he says again.

"But I was right, right?"

"Who cares?"

"I care," I say.

He slaps his forehead and shakes his head again.

"It's not like I planned it or anything," I say. "I—I—I couldn't think." I turn to Debbie. "I couldn't. My brain froze up."

"Of course, Lemonade." Debbie touches my arm. "What a frightening experience. I would have been terrified."

"I was scared for sure," I say to her, and then turn to Charlie. "But then I remembered what you said about him being more scared of me. And he was, Charlie. He really was."

"Are you sure it wasn't someone in a suit?" Tobin glares at me with his arms crossed.

"Very funny," I say. "But you know what? You can ask me that, and I don't even care. You want to know why? Because it was real." I look at Charlie and then at Debbie. "A real live being. With eyes and a nose and even black fingernails."

"Black fingernails?" Debbie repeats.

"Yeah," I say. "And crooked toenails, too."

Tobin huffs a loud sigh.

"I can't believe you saw one." He looks straight at me. "Before me! I'm the founder and president of Bigfoot Detectives Inc. You're just the assistant. It isn't fair."

"Well, maybe it's time to change that," I say.

"Change what?"

"My status."

I look at Charlie, and he's giving me a toothy grin. Bigger than any toothy grin I've ever seen on him.

"I like it," Charlie says.

"You do?" I ask.

"Are you kidding? Of course I do!"

Tobin looks back and forth between Charlie and me. Back at me and then at Charlie.

"You're saying you want to be real half-and-half partners?" Tobin asks.

I think about it.

"Fifty-fifty," I say, smiling. "Witt-Sky Bigfoot Detectives Inc."

Tobin studies me.

"That means you're staying?" he asks.

"Yep."

"For good?"

"Yep," I say again.

"Cross your heart?"

"Cross my heart," I say.

"Not going to change your mind?"

"Nope," I say.

"Not going to blow this taco stand?"

"It's a Popsicle stand! A *Popsicle* stand! And no. I'm not going to blow this Popsicle stand."

He leans back in his chair and looks at me for a long time with wrinkled eyebrows.

"How about we just keep it Bigfoot Detectives Inc. and I make you vice president? You can be in charge of the operations . . . *some* of the operations," he says.

"You mean like moving the message pad?" I ask.

"That's a whole different level of security clearance."

I roll my eyes.

"Well? Are you in or not?" he asks.

I think about it.

"Deal," I say, holding out my hand.

He holds out his, and we shake on our new partnership.

"I think a promotion like this deserves some ice cream," Debbie says. "Don't you agree, Charlie?"

Charlie clears his throat a bunch of times before he answers.

"Absolutely," he says.

"Strawberry?" I smile up at Debbie.

"What else?" Debbie grins back at me and places an arm around my shoulders.

"Vanilla," Tobin states flatly.

Debbie and I look at each other and laugh.

"Wait!" Tobin slaps both palms on the table and then darts up and out of the room. The screen door bangs, and we hear his footsteps pound down the porch steps.

"Where in the world is he going?" I ask Debbie. "Oh, wait, I know. I have to sign it in triplicate, right?"

She just smiles and takes a sip from her flowered mug.

Decaf, with more cream than coffee and two teaspoons of sugar.

Charlie pushes his chair back and leans toward the counter. He grabs the big manila envelope, the one full of official papers that Delores Jaworski left at the store. He carefully opens it and pulls out a packet of pages stuck together with a single staple.

"You're really sure?" he asks.

This time I don't even have to think about it.

"I'm sure," I tell him. "I don't want to leave you or Tobin or Debbie or Mrs. Dickerson or Mr. Harold or Scotty or even the Bigfoot."

He smiles, and I smile too. Debbie sniffs and wipes at her eyes with the corner of a folded paper towel. I watch Charlie scribble his name in cursive on the line at the bottom of the page and then slip it back in the envelope. He licks the top and seals it tight.

"It's official, you're stuck with me," he tells me.

I lay my head on his arm and smell the Irish Spring mixed with Old Spice.

"You're stuck with me, too," I say.

"Nothing I want more." He places his large hand gently on my head.

The screen door bangs again, and Tobin is back and all out of breath and lobbing something in my direction.

"Here," he says.

I catch it. I know exactly what it is the minute it touches my hands. I lay it on the table and smooth out all the wrinkles.

A tan safari hat.

Of my very own.

And not just any safari hat. One with hand-painted letters across the brim.

## BIGFOOT DETECTIVES INC.

"When did you—"

"I knew you'd change your mind," he says. "You're Lemonade. You have been all along, you just forgot. I knew you'd find it again."

"Yeah?" I ask.

"Yeah," he says. "Here, let me put it on you."

I get up from my chair, and he pulls the hat down on top of my head and then adjusts the strap until it's so tight I can hardly swallow. We stand there staring at each other with big goofy grins on our faces in our tan safari hats, strapped tight under our chins.

"Lemonade Liberty Witt, I hereby promote you to vice president of Bigfoot Detectives Inc. And I hereby promote you to full-fledged Bigfoot detective. But first, raise your right hand."

"Not again!" I exclaim.

"It's for a whole new level of clearance," he tells me, raising his right hand high in the air.

"Oh," I say, raising mine, too.

"I, Lemonade Liberty Witt, promise with all faith and allegiance to follow all Bigfoot Detectives Inc. protocol herein set forth by Tobin Sky, the founder and president—"

"Give me a break."

"Say it."

I repeat it, but only with another big eye roll about the whole faith and allegiance thing.

*"And I will well and faithfully perform the duties of the office of vice president with Bigfoot Detectives Inc. . . ."*

"What does a wheel well have to do with anything?"

"It's not a wheel well; it's *will well*. That's what soldiers say in their oath."

"I still don't get what a wheel well has to do with it."

"It's not . . . just say it."

*"With a wheel well, I will do the job of vice president with Bigfoot Detectives Inc. . . ."*

Tobin eyes me. "Close enough," he says. *"And . . . I hereby promise not to blab any confidential cryptozoological information, and . . . I promise I won't move the message pad because I still haven't obtained the proper level of clearance."*

I drop my hand. "Come on!"

"All right." He smiles. "I guess you're official."

Charlie and Debbie raise their coffee mugs and cheer.

My fingers touch the brim of the hat.

My very own safari hat.

And I feel myself grinning so hard that my cheeks hurt. "Well? What do you think?" I ask him, posing like I'm searching for the next midtarsal-break footprint.

He peers at me over his wire-rims, studying me like one of his puzzle pieces.

"I think," he says, "it's a perfect fit."

"I think so too," I say. "How about the yellow legal pad? Do I have clearance for that?"

Tobin thinks about it.

"Maybe," he says, and then grabs my arm. "Wait . . . was that the green phone ringing?"

"Tobin Sky, don't you even think about it," Debbie says. "It's nine o'clock at night. The Bigfoot can wait until morning."

"Oh, Mom, time means nothing to the cryptozoologist."

"Well, it means something to the cryptozoologist's mother." She smiles at Charlie.

Tobin huffs a big sigh and then looks at me.

"Oh eight-thirty hours, partner?"

"I'll be there," I say.

"I really hope so this time, because, you know, you have a tendency to be late, and I told you I'm going to have to put that in your employee file. Vice president or not. It's the rules, and without rules—"

"I know, I know, there's anarchy. Don't worry, I'll be there!" I say.

"Should we synchronize?"

"Tobin!"

"Okay, okay."

He smiles at me, and I smile at him, and then we hear it. A call from deep inside the woods.

"*Whooooooooooooo!*"

# ACKNOWLEDGMENTS

First and foremost, I wish to thank my agent, Laurie McLean, for having faith in a story about a Twinkie-eating cryptid stalking the woods of Northern California. Thank you for helping me shape this story into the best it can be and for your guidance and enthusiasm, and especially for making my dream come true. I am also eternally grateful to Emily Easton and the team at Crown for all their hard work and dedication to this story. Thank you, Emily, for falling in love with Lemonade and Tobin and for your excitement to be the one to share their story.

I wish to express my gratitude to all the incredible people involved with the Hamline University writing program. To the professors and guest lecturers alike, you may not know that your words meant the world in my journey to this place, but they did.

Thank you to all my friends and family—there are too many of you to mention by name, but you know who you are. Mom and Dad, thank you for encouraging our love of books from the start. Scott, thank you for being the best big brother anyone could ask for. And to my husband, thank you for always putting my writing first even when it didn't seem practical to do so. And thank you for being as excited about my dream coming true as I am. I love you all.

A special thanks to Dr. Jeff Meldrum for tweaking my anthropological facts with the words that only a professor of anatomy and anthropology would know.

And finally, I would like to express my deepest love and gratitude to Tobin. Your bravery, love, and grace continue to teach me things I never knew I needed to know. You are my heart and truly a gift for which I will forever be grateful. I promised you a Bigfoot adventure, Little Man, and this story is for you.

# WHAT WOULD YOU DO IF A FLYING SAUCER CRASH-LANDED IN YOUR NEIGHBORHOOD?

MELISSA SAVAGE

THE TRUTH ABOUT MARTIANS

Turn the page to join the martian hunt. . . .

# THE CRASH

We wait.

Thunder rolls.

Lightning flashes.

Downstairs, Baby Kay is finally quieting and the creaking of Momma's chair slows some.

And then in a single second comes the loudest thunderclap I've ever heard. It shakes the earth and shatters the desert silence. It's a clap so loud it sounds like it cracked a million-mile crater deep into the center of the whole wide world, and that's when we see a colossal explosion, out in the direction of Foster Ranch. The blast sprays brilliant bits of fire out in a dazzling burst of light toward the heavens.

When I see all that, I duck under the windowsill and Dibs scrambles for cover in the bed under the safety of his sweaty white shield.

"Did you see that?" he says from behind his cotton armor. "Did you?"

"Yeah," I say, peeking back up over the sill.

"That"—Dibs points a single skinny finger out from under the sheet—"wasn't lightning."

I roll my eyes at him. "Didn't I tell you so?"

I watch in amazement as the explosion turns to small specks of light spraying back toward the earth. It's like the fireworks display we saw tonight at the Fourth of July parade in town, but instead of bits of light bursting up high and then falling down, this explosion happens on the ground and shoots straight up in a blazing bouquet.

"Think it's Martians?" Dibs peeks one eye out.

"Nah," I say. "Has to be something else. Maybe someone just goofing off with leftover firecrackers."

"*Firecrackers?*" He gives me a look. "Are you kidding me?"

A cow out in a nearby pasture moans.

Another one answers her.

"Even the *cows* are talking about it," Dibs tells me.

I watch the lights in silence for a long while, seeing the fiery bits burn out in slow motion toward the ground until it's almost all dark again.

"One of us better go and check things out," Dibs says. "And when you do . . . make sure and tell 'em you come in peace."

I snort again and point a thumb out toward the field. "You're off your rocker if you think I'm going out there," I inform him.

"Well, *I'm* sure not doing it."

I watch the light storm until each of the fiery flickers goes mostly all dark and the desert and the ranch and all the fields around us grow quiet again.

Too quiet.

Even the sloppy drops have stopped shearing the grasses and filling the puddles in the muddy drive, the cows have given up and gone back to sleep, and Momma has shushed and rocked just enough until both the sky and the baby have settled.

All the lights have finally flickered out . . . except one.

But it isn't just any light.

It's . . . *green.*

One single green beam.

My fingers stay glued to the rain-soaked sill as I stare out the window, unable to breathe or move or speak, watching as the far-off green light glows dim and then bright, dim and then bright.

Like an eyeball . . . blinking at me.